Is there no escape?

The wolf pack was enormous: fifty huge wolves and at least twenty of the man-wolves. One, bigger than the rest, moved through the pack. Although he walked on his hind legs, his features were still those of a savage wolf. Reaching behind his back, he procured a saw-toothed dagger and then slowly licked his lips. Raising the dagger high, with cold gray light running down the length of the blade, the pack leader pointed at BJ and Liz. Although no words were spoken, the pack surged forward, howling savagely . . .

GEMINI GAME

GEMINI GAME

MICHAEL SCOTT

Copyright © 1993 by Michael Scott.

Published by Troll Communications L.L.C.

Originally published by The O'Brien Press Ltd., Dublin, Ireland.
First published in hardcover in the United States by Holiday House, Inc.

First U.S. paperback edition 1996.

Cover illustration by Shi Chen.

Printed in the United States of America.

10 9 8 7 6 5 4 3 2 1

Library of Congress Cataloging-in-Publication Data
Scott, Michael.
Gemini Game / Michael Scott.
p. cm.
"First published 1993 by the O'Brien Press Ltd., Dublin, Ireland."
Summary: When players of their virtual reality computer game fall into a coma, Liz and BJ O'Connor, teenage owners of a computer games company, flee from the police in an attempt to locate a copy of their game and correct the programming.
ISBN 0-8234-1092-7 (lib. bdg.)   ISBN 0-8167-4271-5 (pbk.)
[1. Science fiction.   2. Computer games—Fiction.   3. Virtual reality—Fiction.
4. Twins—Fiction.   5. Brothers and sisters—Fiction.   6. Fugitives from justice—
Fiction.]   I. Title.
PZ7.S42733Ge   1994   93-39972   CIP   AC
[Fic]—dc20

For Ferdia,
a new addition

Prologue

THE GIRL WAS FIFTEEN YEARS OF AGE. She looked older . . . much older. Her skin, formerly flawless, was now wrinkled and sagging. Deep lines had been etched into her forehead and beneath her wide-open eyes. Her rich chestnut hair was streaked with gray and silver, and bald patches showed through in places where some had fallen out.

A bank of machines was wired to the girl's skull and chest. They controlled her heart rate and breathing while tubes carried liquid food into her system. Only the machines kept her alive.

The monitors blipped softly. Any variation would set off the automatic alarms to bring the medics running. But so far there had been no emergency. Only the machine on the shelf above the bed showed any activity. Narrow leads ran from the squat box to circular patches fixed to the girl's head and spine. A color monitor showed a series of jagged lines and colored pulses. They were the only indication of brain activity.

The girl dreamed while her body slowly died. Occasionally, her mouth would stretch open in a silent scream.

In the next room, a twenty-two-year-old man lay in an identical condition. There was an eight-year-old boy in the room beside him. In the rooms beyond, nine more men, women, and children slept in deep comas. And all of their dreams were terrifying.

1

BJ POUNDED THE KEYBOARD IN FRUSTRATION and shoved it away from him. He'd spent the last two hours trying to compress two megabytes of data into a program less than half that size.

On the giant three-dimensional screen before him, INPUT FAILURE blinked steadily.

He heard the door hiss open behind him but didn't bother to turn around. No one was allowed access to this part of the building except his sister, Liz.

Long arms, tipped with slender fingers, reached over his shoulders and pulled the crescent-shaped keyboard forward. Resting her chin on her brother's head, the girl flicked her fingers across the keys. Figures and symbols flowed down the screen.

"I've tried that," BJ muttered. "It won't work."

Liz pressed enter.

The screen flickered. INPUT ACCEPTED.

"What won't work?" the girl demanded.

"Thanks, Liz," BJ breathed. "I was afraid I'd have to start all over again." He stretched, taut muscles cracking. "You're back early."

"We have a problem," Liz said quietly, "a very serious problem."

BJ swung around to look at his sister. BJ and Liz were twins, but only their eyes—the color of cold stone—matched. BJ was short and bulky but, at fifteen, Liz was already standing at six feet. BJ would never grow any taller than five foot five. He was completely bald, his smooth face, round eyes, and small mouth giving him a permanently surprised expression. Liz's face was harder, sharper, the cheekbones clearly defined, her eyes slightly slanted. Like most computer programmers, the girl wore her hair cropped tight.

"What's wrong?" BJ asked.

"We're in trouble," she said very softly.

BJ turned to look at his sister. Liz was standing by the window, gazing down on the sprawling city. It was still early morning and the sulphurous yellow smog hadn't thickened to the point where it wiped out all the details of streets and buildings. Within the hour, the air would be an unbreathable poisonous soup, blanketing the streets below in yellow acid fog.

Liz turned and sat down in the contoured chair before her giant screen, her fingers dancing lightly across the smooth surface of her own crescent-shaped keyboard.

"How much trouble?" BJ asked. His chair moved across the room on a cushion of air and settled down beside hers.

"Watch," she said softly.

Graphics swirled on the screen and music swelled. As the first organ note rumbled out, BJ's face lit up with a smile. *Night's Castle!*

The twins were Game Makers, computer programmers who specialized in making ever more complicated and realistic games. It had taken them nearly two years to create and program the computer-generated world of *Night's Castle.* Research costs had run into the millions, but they knew they'd make it back on sales of the game. Gemini Corporation, the company they had inherited from their parents, was the world leader in the games market. Sales of their titles ran into hundreds of millions. A *Reader's Digest* survey claimed that every home in the civilized world had at least one Gemini Corporation game; most had two or more.

BJ's cold gray eyes took in all the details of the three-dimensional screen, noting the colors and shapes. Everything seemed in order. "What's wrong with *Night's Castle?*"

Liz closed the game and called up the electronic mail. URGENT flashed in three-inch-high red letters. At the bottom of the screen was the stylized badge of the police section, Department 13. BJ straightened in his chair. Department 13 looked after computer-related crimes. Suddenly he felt ill. "We've had a game failure," he said, imagining the worst.

"Worse!"

"Worse?" he whispered. "There's nothing worse than game failure!"

Liz opened the urgent file. Blinking letters crawled across the screen.

ALL SALES OF NIGHT'S CASTLE BANNED
ILLEGAL GAME
TWELVE PLAYERS CRITICAL IN VR COMA
BJ & LIZ O'CONNOR REPORT TO THIS OFFICE IMMEDIATELY

"An illegal game!" BJ attempted a laugh, but it came out as a shaky cough. "This is ridiculous. We tested every step of *Night's Castle* ourselves. I practically lived in that game for the past three months!"

Liz nodded. She eased herself back in her chair, which adjusted to accommodate her body form. "I know. But over the past two days, twelve people—men, women, and children—from different backgrounds, races, and cultures have slipped into a deep coma-like sleep. The only connection between them was that they were all playing *Night's Castle* when it happened."

"Oh my God!"

"Department 13 considers it an illegal game," she said. "And you know what that means."

BJ swallowed hard. "What are we going to do?" he wondered aloud.

"The police want us to report to them voluntarily. If we don't, then they'll come looking for us."

BJ shook his head. "I'm not surrendering myself to the police."

"Neither am I," Liz agreed, her fingers moving across the keyboard, quickly accessing the computers that regulated the city's traffic flow. Sensors recorded the passage of all vehicles past various points, and the owner was charged accordingly. The more a driver used a particular road, the more he or she paid. At any time a driver's whereabouts could be checked. Although the information was meant to be highly confidential, the twins used the latest in computer technology to crack the codes, giving them access to every other computer network across the city.

Streams of digits began to flow down the screen.

"This is the traffic in all the streets surrounding this building," Liz said, her fingers calling up the location of all official vehicles nearby.

Six rows of numbers remained on the enormous screen.

"Police," BJ whispered.

"Six cars," Liz said, calling up another program, which showed a map of the city. Then she mixed both programs, superimposing the police vehicles on the map. The cars were closing in fast, converging on Gemini Corporation's headquarters. Liz stabbed a single button, clearing the screen. "We need to buy some time to investigate *Night's Castle*. We'll have to prove that there's nothing wrong with the game, but if we're locked up we won't have that chance."

The vehicles stopped in a ragged line directly outside the building. The police had arrived.

"Hold them off," Liz said urgently, "while I collect a few things."

BJ turned back to his own machine. Everything in the enormous building was computer-controlled . . . and BJ controlled the large mainframe computer in the basement that regulated the light and heat for every room on the fifty floors. It also operated the main door, waste disposal, and laundry. It took BJ less than half a minute to tap into the computer's command program and delete the line of code covering the front door. He then rerouted a little of the building's power into the call button beneath Gemini Corporation's nameplate.

"All set," he called.

BJ flicked on the overhead scanner allowing him to see down into the porch. A dozen black-clad police officers were huddled in the doorway, sheltering from the poisonous rain. Their breathing masks made them look like giant insects. He saw one man step forward to trace the names beneath the dozens of buttons. He stopped halfway down, jabbed that of Gemini Corporation. There was an explosion of sparks and the officer was flung backward, tumbling another four men with him onto the ground. Black smoke coiled from the remains of the button.

Liz ran out of her room, stuffing items into a black carryall. She stopped to see what her brother was doing. "You always go too far," she said, shaking her head in annoyance. "You could have just locked the doors. You know what's going to happen now, don't you?"

He shook his head.

"They're going to shoot the door off its hinges."

"They'll never do that," BJ said confidently.

Fifty stories below, an officer pointed an ugly wide-mouthed pistol at the door. The twins couldn't hear the bang, but the whole door disintegrated in an explosion of glass and molten metal.

"Let's get out of here," BJ whispered. Stepping back from his computer terminal, he shouted, "Secure." All the machines immediately shut down. They would start up again only when the twins voiced a coded command.

Before the police had recovered from the explosion, BJ and Liz were sliding down the ventilation shafts leading into the heart of the building. They knew this way by heart—after all, they had designed the building. The shafts came out at the rear of a narrow service alleyway. The twins stopped in the parking lot in the sub-basement to collect their masks, goggles, and metal-foil rain slickers from the trunk of their car. They realized they couldn't take the vehicle: the police would be able to track them with the traffic computers.

A minute later, the twins were hurrying out into the early morning air. Visibility was down to about ten yards and their wrist monitors blinked red, indicating that the air was already too poisonous to breathe. Less than an hour previously they had been among the richest people in the world; now they were fugitives from the law.

2

CAPTAIN EDDIE LYONS HATED THE TWINS. He envied their immense fortune, their talent, and their fame. They were young, rich, and successful; they were everything he wasn't. But all that was about to change.

The big, bulky police officer in the black foil raincoat stepped through the smoking ruin of the door and strode toward the elevator followed by half his officers. The remainder darted toward the stairs. They weren't going to allow the twins to escape. As Captain Lyons stepped into the elevator, his thin lips twisted in a grim smile. He had waited a long time for this day.

Eddie Lyons had been a police officer for twenty years, and for the last seven he had been in charge of Department 13. This department specialized in licensing and policing the new generation of computer games, the type the twins created: the virtual reality games.

It was a job he hated. But he remained in it because it gave him a chance to control the Game Makers, the programmers who supplied the virtual reality industry, and he hated those even more.

The first computer games had been crude and basic. As

the hardware improved, so did the games. Eventually computers appeared that did nothing but play games. In the last few years of the twentieth century, when technology was developing at an extraordinary rate, the games machines often led the way with new ideas, new directions.

There had been attempts at creating virtual reality games in the 1990s. Heavy, cumbersome helmets allowed players to see a vaguely three-dimensional, though not very realistic, world. The player wore a glove that appeared in the virtual reality world as a pointing hand. The player became part of the game.

Technology improved. Soon the helmets had shrunk to spectacles and the heavy gloves became soft and flexible. In the first few years of the new century, computer users wore bands across their heads with soft pressure pads resting on the temples, just behind the eyes. The computer images were now pulsed directly into the user's skull. Graphics became more and more realistic. Photographic images could be entered into a computer program and then animated. Eventually, it was possible for the user to become part of any number of programs, either educational or entertainment.

Naturally, there were always those who sought to make a profit from the new programs. Violent and disturbing games appeared, demanding hours and sometimes days of the players' time. Some games implanted commands that forced the hypnotized player to commit crimes.

And so the VR police were formed. Their job was to monitor the flood of virtual reality games, assess those which might be dangerous, and investigate VR-related crimes. Lyons commanded a staff of fifty officers, who were among the brightest programmers in the world. Indeed, many of the university computer courses sent their students to train with Department 13—the VR police.

Lyons had been following the twins' progress since they had first entered the game-making field a couple of years ago. He had immediately realized that their games were very different from the general run. The VR worlds they created were far more real than most of the others, and the attention to detail was incredible. When they were starting out, the twins had contented themselves with the ever-popular treasure-hunt type games, aimed at young teenagers. But their last few games had been far more complex and definitely aimed at the adult market.

Two years ago Lyons had graded one of their games, *Magician's Law,* SAO (Strictly Adult Only) and had attempted to remove certain scenes he considered too violent. But neither he nor his top programmers had been able to crack the code to gain access to the program itself.

Eventually, Lyons had been forced to ask the twins to remove the scenes from the game. They had refused, saying there was no need to censor it since he had given it an SAO sticker restricting it to adults.

Lyons had been furious: no Game Maker had ever defied him before. But there was nothing he could do. He was even more annoyed when he learned that the game had gone on to sell more than one hundred million copies worldwide. The twins had designed all their games in such a way that they could not be copied unofficially. Any attempt to do so caused the disc to overheat and melt inside the machine, ruining not only the game but also the machine itself. One player had sued because his machine had been ruined; the twins simply sued him in turn and won, because his attempt to copy their material was illegal.

But Lyons had been patient. Sooner or later, he knew, the twins would slip up. He put a twenty-four-hour watch on them. He knew where they lived, what they ate, where they shopped, what music they listened to, and the clothes they wore. He was convinced that they were up to no good and he was determined to destroy them.

However, he didn't think he would be coming after them so soon. Two days ago, he had lost one of his best men to the twins' latest game, *Night's Castle.* The man had been playing it when he had suddenly fallen into a deep sleep in front of his machine. Doctors diagnosed a VR coma. Lyons immediately requested details on all citizens who had fallen into similar comas over the last couple of days. By dawn he had reports of a dozen people all across the country who were affected. In each case, the police had discovered a copy of *Night's Castle* in the victim's machine.

He had them! Creation and distribution of an illegal game meant that the twins would lose their fortune and spend a long time in a virtual reality prison. He smiled: that, he thought, was an appropriate punishment.

The elevator hummed to a stop on the fiftieth floor but the outer doors refused to open. SECURITY CLEARANCE flashed on the narrow screen over them.

Lyons pressed his badge against the lock, allowing the light to scan its code. Police Department badges opened any door.

ACCESS DENIED.

Lyons blinked at the screen. That was impossible! He pressed his badge against the lock once more. A pale green light scanned it.

ACCESS DENIED.

Wondering if his badge was dirty or damaged, Lyons snatched a badge from the officer to his left and pressed it against the lock. The doors still refused to open. "They must have changed the codes," he muttered. By modifying the lock, the twins had committed yet another crime.

"Ground floor," he said aloud.

The elevator obediently returned to the ground floor. As he stepped out into the marbled hall, his collar radio buzzed. "Report," he snapped.

"We cannot gain entrance to the twin's floor from the stairs." The officer's voice echoed flatly through the tiny speaker. "The security codes have been altered. However, we have scanned the floor and we're picking up no signs of life. They must have slipped out as we were coming up."

"Cancel the operation. Report back to the station." Lyons strode back to his car in a foul mood. He climbed in, forgetting to brush off the harsh-smelling rain, which immediately began to burn through the plastic seats. However, it gave him some satisfaction to place BJ's and Liz's names on the most wanted list. In police stations and patrol cars all across the city, their pictures and personal details were flashed onto officers' screens. Lyons ran his hand through his thinning hair, knowing it would only be a matter of time before they would be caught. In the computer-controlled and monitored world of the twenty-first century, there was no place to hide.

22

3

"SUBWAY," BJ MUTTERED, his voice muffled by the breathing mask. He pointed into the gloom to the pulsing green light that marked the location of the underground rail network.

Liz nodded; she had just been about to suggest the same thing. They needed to put as much distance as possible between themselves and Lyons. Once he put their names on the wanted list, their credit cards would be automatically canceled, preventing them from eating, drinking, or moving.

The first set of sliding doors shuddered open as they approached. Huge extraction fans in the walls and ceiling began cleaning the air as they walked the ten yards to the second set of doors, which opened and shut behind them. It was safe at this point to take off the breathing masks, but most people preferred to pass through the third set of doors before they risked breathing the air.

Liz pushed back her hood and pulled off her mask, then scratched her head vigorously. The metallic material in the hood irritated the skin.

A dozen people milled around the automated ticket

machines. BJ watched them closely, but they seemed eager to purchase their tickets and be on their way, none of them lingering suspiciously. Two tourists consulted the glowing map on the wall beside the machine, tapping in their destination, then watching their route light up on the map.

"Keep watch," Liz muttered. She slid her metal card into the slot and tapped in the first destination that came to mind. A sliver of plastic dropped into the ticket slot. Relieved that their credit cards hadn't already been canceled, she quickly tapped in another dozen destinations all across the city. She knew Lyons would run a check on their credit cards, calling up all their recent accounts. With so many different locations to confuse him, she hoped they would have time to escape. She glanced over her shoulder. "By the way, where are we going?"

"West Central," BJ murmured.

"What's in West Central?" she wondered aloud, tapping in the station, which was on the other side of the city. Two slivers of plastic spat out of the machine. She gathered up the handful of plastic tickets and pushed them into her pockets.

"West Central's the nearest stop to the Quays," BJ said, as if that explained everything. Liz followed her brother down the sharply sloping escalator to the subway line, wondering why he wanted to go to the Quays.

The Quays were the oldest part of the city. Liz had read that a river had once run through there and that the quayside had extended for miles in either direction, right down to the sea. At some time in the past—she wasn't sure when—the river had been diverted and channeled underground. The exposed river bed had been built upon, but the money had run out, leaving a two-mile-long section unfinished.

Into the half-completed warren of buildings and factories, office blocks, and shops had moved the poor, the down-and-outs, the criminals and those who objected to the ever-present government looking over their shoulders. The Quays were wild and lawless. Paper and metal coinage were still used and many of the citizens went armed. Citizens of the Quays paid no taxes and obeyed no law. In return, however, they received none of the benefits of the city dwellers: no health care, no food, no education, and the police were rarely seen. Liz nodded. She knew now why BJ had suggested the Quays.

The twins slowed as they approached the automatic ticket gates. If the police had accessed their records and canceled the tickets they had purchased in the past few minutes, they were trapped.

Glancing sidelong at her brother, Liz shoved the first sliver of plastic into the slot.

The gate hummed open.

Once they were through, Liz quickly slid the remainder of the cards into the machine. Now, when the police called up their credit-card records, they'd have over a dozen places to choose from.

"So far so good," BJ murmured, sweat glistening on his bald head.

"Do you have any idea what we're going to do?" Liz asked as they stepped out onto the platform.

"I'm working on it."

The early morning rush was over and the platform was almost deserted. A couple of tourists stood at one end, conspicuous with their camera and vids. Two construction workers, their metallic overalls stained with the corrosive acid rain, sat on the battered metal seats. At the other end of the platform, a group of youths squatted around a portable sound blaster pulsing out old-fashioned technorock.

BJ grinned at his sister. "There's nothing like the sound of good old rock 'n' roll . . ."

"And that's *nothing* like the sound of good old rock 'n' roll," she finished with a smile.

A green light flickered along the walls, barely visible beneath the sprayed graffiti, indicating that a train was coming.

"We'll take the first train that comes," BJ said, "and change at the next station."

Liz nodded. She glanced at the wall map of the underground. The green line went through the heart of the city, whereas West Central was on the blue line. "We should stay on for two stops," she said. "Then when we change trains it will be a straight run to West Central."

BJ's reply was drowned out in the rush of foul air as the subway train came into the station, its leaking hoverbags screaming with escaping gas. The doors opened and a dozen people got off, most of them pulling up their hoods and adjusting their goggles as they prepared to go back out into the street.

BJ and Liz chose one of the middle cars, trying to find seats that weren't too badly scarred. There were about twenty people in their subway car. Most were idly watching the advertisements flickering above the windows, but BJ noticed a young couple playing a hand-held computer game. The sleek black console bore the golden Gemini Corporation logo. He nudged his sister as she sat down beside him and nodded toward the pair. Liz followed the direction of his look and nodded in understanding. She tilted her head to one side, listening, finally identifying a snatch of the game's music.

"Death's Law," she murmured.

BJ's smile broadened. The Law games had always been his favorites, even though they were now considered old-fashioned.

There was a disturbance at the other end of the car as the group of youths who had been in the station shoved their way onto the train, their sound blaster throbbing. As BJ watched, a tall, skinny youth in a tattered army uniform put the fat box on the floor and slid the volume control all the way up to max. The car echoed with the sound, making speech—and even thought—impossible. The youths, both male and female, gathered round the sound blaster, daring anyone to interfere with it. In the aisle, two young women and one of the older boys began to dance, a shuddering, shivering motion that looked as if they were having a seizure.

Liz turned to watch the couple who had been playing the console game. The young man was struggling to rise to his feet, but the woman was holding him back. As she shook her head, pleading with him not to interfere, Liz noticed a baby strapped to a carrier across the woman's breast. The child's face was screwed up into a knot, and although she couldn't hear it, Liz knew the child was screaming, terrified by the noise. Liz looked at her brother but he too was staring at the baby. The twins turned their heads at the same time and looked at the youths.

BJ patted his pockets beneath the rain slicker, looking for something.

Liz saw his smile and glanced down as he pulled out a palm-sized circular disc. With the edge of his fingernail, he peeled away the plastic covering to expose the coiled wires beneath. She frowned. It was a compact disc cleaner. BJ had developed it as a quick way of formatting and cleaning the small microcompact discs on which they stored information and games. Information written to the discs was impossible to remove—until BJ had discovered that less than a tenth of a second of a high-voltage electrical charge would permanently erase all the data on it, making it reusable. The twins thought they might market the idea until one of their accountants reminded them that Gemini Corporation owned a company making compact discs. If they were reusable, sales would drop. Now, BJ used the cleaner only for his personal discs.

When he had exposed the coiled wiring, BJ separated two of the hair-thin wires and snapped them in half, exposing the metal cores. Then he thumbed the ON switch and a red LED on the top of the disc began blinking, counting back to zero. When it reached zero the LED changed to green. BJ leaned over and pressed the two exposed wires to the metal mesh in the floor. Liz watched as a spark leaped from the wires onto the metal and then raced down the floor.

The sound blaster burst apart in an explosion of sparks,

showering the youths with red-hot pieces of plastic and splinters of metal. The stench of melting plastic filled the train.

The silence that followed was almost deafening. Then the baby screamed. At about the same time someone laughed. The youths' shivering dance had turned into a wild cavorting as they attempted to pluck spots of melted plastic off their skin and clothing.

Liz nudged her brother. "Our stop," she murmured.

4

IT HAD TAKEN THE TECHNICAL SQUAD sent by Captain Lyons the better part of two hours to realize they could not bypass the security locks on the twins' apartment. Lyons, who had come back from the police station, finally ordered cutting equipment to slice the door in half. He was watching the thin blue flame cut through the metal when his sergeant tapped him on the shoulder.

"We've traced them, sir!"

"Let me see that!" Captain Lyons snatched the tiny screen from his sergeant's hand and looked at the rapidly scrolling list of figures. According to this, the twins had bought tickets almost two hours earlier for fourteen separate locations all across the city.

Lyons ran his blunt finger down the pressure-sensitive screen. The figures shivered and disappeared and were replaced by the image of one of his VR officers back at headquarters.

"Report," Lyons snapped.

"All the tickets have gone through the machines so we can assume that they are on the subway." Lyons watched as the image shimmered with interference, the colors bleeding into one another. "We haven't canceled the credit cards, but we have put a priority trace on them. The next time they're used, we'll know immediately."

Lyons nodded. He folded the screen and handed it back to his sergeant. The twins had escaped. This wasn't going to look good on his record, though in a curious way he was actually pleased. When he had first brought forward the idea that Gemini Corporation was making illegal games, most of the other officers in Department 13, including his superiors, had laughed at him. But they had been forced to reconsider when he had shown the connection between the players who fell into a VR coma and Gemini Corporation's *Night's Castle*. Some officers had defended the twins, suggesting that it was probably nothing more than an accident or a coincidence. The fact that the twins had gone on the run supported his theory that they were guilty.

The door finally gave way, falling back into the apartment in a shower of sparks and gray-white smoke. Lyons strode forward across the twisted metal, grimacing with pain as the heat burned through his boots. He walked around the apartment that took up the entire fiftieth floor of Gemini Corporation's building. He wondered what space like this would cost to rent. He himself lived in a one-bedroom box on the other side of the city that cost half his salary every month.

His technicians and programmer swarmed over the computer equipment. It was all state-of-the-art, the latest designs from Japan and Korea, including a few new variations and designs he had never seen before. And it was all useless to him. None of his highly trained technicians could even turn the machines on.

"Security-coded," one of his officers reported. "Probably keyed to the twins' own voice patterns. They're the only people who can activate the machines for you."

"Couldn't we take out the memory core and fit it into our own machines?"

The technician shook his head doubtfully. "If they've gone to this much trouble to safeguard their data, I'd guess they've booby-trapped the memory. Any attempt to interfere with it will completely blank the discs." The man shrugged his shoulders. "You'll have to ask the twins."

"Oh, I will," Lyons said fiercely. "I will." He turned away and leaned against the window, staring down at the lemon-yellow blanket of cloud that covered the city. Brightly lit skyscrapers broke through the cloud, like islands rising out of a sea. He rested his forehead against the cool plastic and looked down at the cloud again, wishing he could see through it. Where were they? And why were they running?

There was nowhere to hide.

5

"DO YOU WANT TO TELL ME what we're doing here?" Liz demanded. They had entered the Quays ten minutes earlier, and she was becoming increasingly nervous about the strange characters in the dirty narrow streets. In the city center everyone wore metallic rain slickers, but here people dressed in a variety of shawls, wraps, cloaks, and coats. Their goggles and breathing apparatus had been modified and painted so that they looked like grotesque masks. Liz felt that she and her brother were conspicuous in their clean silver slickers and mirrored goggles.

"Not so loud!" BJ caught his sister's arm and pulled her across to what he thought was a derelict building, until he discovered a dozen pairs of eyes staring at him out of the gloom. Light flared in the shadows, revealing a group of children, none older than ten. They were gaunt with hunger, and BJ didn't like the way they were staring at him so intently. He suddenly remembered the rumors about some inhabitants of the Quays turning to cannibalism.

They walked on until they discovered a fast-food restaurant. Its pressure doors opened and closed with solid thumps, indicating that they were kept in good repair. But the interior of the restaurant, like just about everything else they had seen of the Quays, was shabby and unclean.

While Liz found seats, BJ dialed up two small bottles of purified water from the dispenser, paying for it with one of the few plastic notes he possessed. He counted his change carefully and realized that the water had cost nearly three times as much as in the city.

"Now, tell me," Liz said as he sat down across from her. "What are we doing here?"

BJ ran his hands across his bald head and scratched furiously. He tasted the water and discovered that it wasn't as bad as he'd expected. Leaning across the chipped table, he looked into his sister's troubled face. "This is one of the few places the police will have difficulty following us," he began. "No credit cards are accepted on the Quays, so Lyons can't trace us that way."

"But surely there are police informers here," Liz said, glancing around the restaurant. None of the customers seemed to be paying any special attention to them.

"I know that. I know we can't stay free indefinitely. We've got two or maybe three days at most before they catch us."

Liz nodded in agreement. She twisted the cap on her bottle of water, watching as the sell-by seal turned a deep red, indicating that the date had expired. Ignoring the warning, she sipped it carefully, discovering it tasted foul and metallic. "Is all the food in here like this?" she whispered.

"I don't think we'll have much chance to find out," BJ said with a grin.

"Why not?" She took another sip of water.

He opened his hand and showed her how little money he had. "That's all we've got left. We don't have enough to buy any more food."

Liz shook her head in astonishment. "What have we achieved by running away? Why didn't we stay and have the lawyers fight our case?"

BJ shrugged. "You know how powerful Department 13 is, and Captain Lyons is not exactly a friend. He's been waiting for an opportunity like this for a long time."

"So what have we got?" Liz asked. "Three days of freedom . . ."

"Maybe two," BJ said.

"Maybe two. In those two days we've got to find ourselves a corrupted copy of the *Night's Castle* game. We've got to discover what's wrong with it and correct the mistake . . . and while we're doing all this, we've got nowhere to stay and nothing to eat."

BJ nodded. "That's about right."

Liz forced herself to drink the remainder of the water. She'd read somewhere that water was now recycled one hundred and twenty times; she was beginning to think that this bottle had slipped through the purification system. Watching her brother's face, she could tell that he had a plan and was bursting to tell her. To annoy him, she deliberately looked away, glancing around the restaurant. There were two other couples sitting at the small circular tables, deeply engrossed in conversation. A child sat on the floor beside one of the couples. Liz looked at the girl's face, trying to guess her age. Beneath the dirt and the deeply etched lines, she looked no more than fourteen or fifteen. The Quays were less than a mile from their offices—and yet it was another world. Liz suddenly felt very frightened.

BJ couldn't contain himself any longer. "I've got a plan," he whispered.

"I know," Liz said tiredly. "So tell me about it."

✳   ✳   ✳

They found the Gaming Hall easily enough. It was a brightly lit oasis in the middle of a dingy street, red, yellow, and green light flickering from a rotating laser sign proclaiming THE GAMES MASTER.

The building had once been a warehouse. It was enormous, and the noise and heat inside were incredible. Row after row of multicolored plastic gaming machines and miniature arcade games took up the entire first floor. The air was alive with bells and whistles, high-pitched buzzing, screams, shouts, and electronic sound effects. In most cases, the games were played by a single person, who stood or sat in front of the machine, staring intently at the glowing three-dimensional images while fingers jabbed and punched at button combinations.

BJ curled his lip dismissively. "Kids' stuff," he sneered.

The next level down was far quieter. The lighting was dull and muted, glowing strips in the floor leading the way to the VR games. Old-fashioned helmet games were still available for newcomers to the VR gaming world, but for the more experienced players, glove and goggle combinations were available.

"What are we looking for?" Liz asked.

"I don't know yet," BJ said quietly. "Let's take a look at this."

In the center of a circular arena, in a pool of soft orange light, a trio of players fought against one another. The players, two young men and a young girl, lay on soft foam beds. Semicircular bands around their heads were attached to outsize circular goggles. The players' hands, encased in soft leather gloves that trailed sensors into a video display unit, were moving, waving wildly back and forth. Their heads were twisting as the computer graphics were fed directly onto their optic nerves and full stereo sound was vibrated straight into their brains. For the benefit of those watching, the game with its three players was projected onto a rotating screen above the arena.

"Now, this is more like it," BJ said, leaning on the rail, looking from the players to the screen and back again, matching the players with their onscreen images.

The game was Meteors, one of the most popular group VR games. In it, the players were faced with a meteor storm, which they had to pass through without being hit more than twice. Their only defenses were three small circular shields, which they could use to knock the meteors away. Part of the game strategy, however, was to push the meteors toward the opposing players.

Liz nudged her brother. "The girl is good."

BJ nodded. The girl was going to win. He looked from the screen—where she had sent a flaming meteorite into her nearest opponent, eliminating him—to the couch where the girl's body lay. She was small and slender, her features vaguely Oriental. She was completely bald except for a long tail of hair that ran down the center of her skull and onto her back. Most VR players shaved their heads, since hair sometimes interfered with the contact of

37

the VR bands to the skull. He turned back to the screen just as the girl dodged a meteor, which broke up into dozens of pieces. She caught one of the pieces on the edge of her shield and sent it skimming back into her nearest rival. He exploded in a ball of fire. A few minutes more and she had outmaneuvered her second opponent.

GAME OVER flashed up in letters of fire.

There was a ragged cheer from the onlookers. The two young men sat up and pulled off their goggles and headbands, blinking dizzily as their eyes and senses adjusted to the real world after all the artificial data they had been fed.

A small, stout man hurried into the center of the arena. BJ thought at first that he was wearing a ragged suit that had seen better days, but then he realized that the rents and tears were probably fashionable. The man looked up at the audience gathered around the arena, and his voice boomed from hidden microphones.

"Now, ladies and gentlemen, you've seen the game. How would you like to experience it for yourselves? The thrills, the spills of a real meteor storm. You'll really believe you're there. It's only ten units a game and, as a special bonus," he added, pulling out a sheaf of plastic money, "one hundred units to the player who can defeat Ariel." He waved his arm at the girl, who still hadn't removed her helmet or goggles.

"Is she good?" Liz asked a wild-haired, white-faced girl standing beside her.

"You really don't know?" The girl looked surprised. Liz shook her head. The girl smiled, showing teeth that had been filed to razor-sharp points. "Ariel's the best. She's never been defeated. I hear she lives in that VR world; that's why she's so good at it." She pointed to a glowing panel on the wall above Ariel's head. It showed the numeral 330. As they watched, it changed to 332. "That's how many she's defeated at Meteors. Most of the VR games around here have what they call an Ariel Number above them."

BJ leaned forward and nudged his sister. "Maybe you should give it a try," he suggested.

"You'd be wasting your money," the white-faced girl said.

"Have we got ten units?" Liz asked her brother.

He pulled out a handful of metal-rimmed plastic coins and counted them. "Eleven," he said.

As she was picking out the ten coins, BJ looked into Liz's cold gray eyes. "Don't lose," he whispered, "or else we won't eat tonight."

She nodded. "I'll try. But she's good."

"But you're better. You're the Game Maker."

6

LIZ LAY ON THE NARROW BED and placed the goggles on her face.

There was a single moment of nausea while the colors crackled across her eyes and her head felt as if ants were crawling around inside her skull. Then the images settled and she found she was standing on a rock in the midst of cold, empty space. She was dressed in a one-piece silver suit, and there was a small circular shield on her left arm. Two similar shields were attached to her belt. Turning her head to the left, she could see that Ariel, standing on a similar rock, was dressed identically, except that her suit was a dull golden color. The girl was smaller than she'd expected, with a thin, sharp face. Her eyes were sunk deep into her skull and completely black, without pupil or white.

Liz turned back to the cold emptiness of space. She knew that what she was seeing was nothing more than a computer-generated image projected onto her retina by the goggles and headband, which also supplied the sound. But the whole creation was so vivid, so real, that it was very easy to believe in the illusion.

A glowing fireball grew in the air above her head, then exploded into colored streamers of fire. The game was about to begin.

METEORS: CONTESTANTS READY

The first level was straightforward enough.

Liz stood on the rock and dodged the stones that came hurtling out of space at her. Twice she struck them with her shield, and once she actually managed to send a fragment of rock spinning toward Ariel. The girl knocked it aside with ease. Liz dodged another rock that hummed by her head, leaving a trail of sparks in its wake. She shattered a second on her shield, closing her eyes as burning cinders of rock spun around her. When she opened them again, instinct made her turn to the left. Her left arm shot up automatically, catching the fragment of stone Ariel had bounced at her. Although she managed to deflect the rock, she was slightly off balance and the next meteor exploded in the center of her chest, bathing her in cold, red fire.

The sky flashed red and her shield crumbled to dust.

One life down.

Liz slid the second shield off her belt and slipped it onto her wrist. OK; she was getting the feel of the game now. The computer generated random numbers of meteors. She wondered if the stones were deliberately fired at the two players or were merely shot from one end of the screen to the other so that if the players happened to be standing in the way—then, tough!

The sky changed color and the game began again.

Liz concentrated on the pattern of the meteors, counting the numbers and the way they spread out. She discovered that the stones were simply sent from one end of the screen to the other. Instead of trying to stop all the meteors, what she had to do was avoid the stones coming directly at her and concentrate on those that Ariel managed to spin off at her. Planting her feet firmly on the rock, she moved her body, twisting to allow the stones to buzz past and occasionally striking out at one, trying to send it toward Ariel.

As the game went on it speeded up. The meteors now trailed multicolored flames, and what looked like tiny pebbles spun after them. A trio of burning stones suddenly appeared before Liz. She dodged the first and shattered the second on her shield and then just about managed to bring her shield down as the third stone raced in. She clipped the edge, breaking the stone into a dozen pieces, sending them all toward Ariel. The small girl managed to deflect three of the burning pieces, but the fourth stone shattered her shield. Before she could get to another shield, two stones struck her, knocking her to her feet.

One life down.

Ariel came to her feet and pulled on her second shield. She turned her head to stare at Liz, who was shocked by the expression of hatred that twisted the girl's thin sharp face. Liz abruptly realized that this was more than a game to Ariel.

The next round introduced an extra difficulty. The ragged clump of rock they were standing on began to revolve, turning slowly beneath their feet. Liz staggered and almost lost her balance just as the first flaming meteors appeared. They started as colored specks in the blackness of space, then rapidly grew into large, fiery balls. The meteors were bigger than any she had faced before. Instead of flying by in a solid clump, they burst apart when they were directly in front of the two girls, spraying them with jagged lumps of burning stone.

The first explosion caught Liz by surprise. She reacted instinctively, hitting out at the stones instead of calmly dodging them. Two stones struck her shield at the same time, destroying it in a cloud of silver dust. Another fragment of stone ricocheted off the ground at her feet and hit her low in the stomach. Then she felt a violent blow on the back of her head, driving her to her knees.

Another life down.

As she crouched on the ground she realized that Ariel must have sent a shot spinning toward her. Shaking her head to clear it, she stood up and pulled on her last shield. She glanced sidelong at the smaller girl. Her thin lips were twisted into a smirk. Liz deliberately turned away. She crouched forward, awaiting the next wave of meteors, desperately trying to work out a strategy. If she had made the game, how would she have programmed it?

Tiny colored specks appeared in the distance as the meteors raced toward her.

This was basically a very simple computer game. It had been given a new look because of the virtual reality software, which allowed the player to be inside the game, but, Liz realized, that still didn't change the rules.

So how *would* she have programmed the game? In her mind's eye, she saw the long lines of computer code that would make up the program. She had to bite the inside of her cheek to keep herself from smiling when she realized that they matched up with the way the game had been progressing. She visualized the next dozen lines of computer code . . . and immediately knew what was going to happen next, how the game would react. The meteor would appear there and explode just there . . .

Liz was moving before the first scattering of meteors exploded. They whooshed past her but none touched. Her left hand shot out once . . . twice . . . again . . . sending three fragments of burning rock toward Ariel, timing it so that they would be coming at her just as a meteor burst in front of her. The smaller girl froze for a single second, undecided between the two threats . . . and was showered in a dozen red-hot clumps of stone.

Another life down.

Each player was now down to a single life. The next round would be the deciding one. Liz wasn't sure which of them had the advantage. Ariel had played the game before. She was experienced and knew what was coming next while Liz could only guess, based upon her knowledge of similar games. But Liz knew that Ariel had never been so close to defeat before: that would put her under extra pressure.

Four meteors appeared in a diamond formation.

Liz ran the code in her head, quickly deciding that, when the meteors exploded, the only way to escape their deadly rain would be to leap through the middle, hoping she would be able to keep her feet on the moving rock.

The meteors burst in a clockwise sequence, starting with the topmost stone. Each rock broke up into four smaller stones, so suddenly that there were sixteen buzzing toward them trailing multicolored fire.

Liz waited patiently, concentrating on the pattern. There would only be one chance . . .

Now!

She jumped up through the gap in the rocks, landed squarely on her feet, spun, and struck two of the stones from behind with her shield.

Caught by surprise, Ariel managed to destroy the first stone on her shield but couldn't stop the second from shattering against her arm.

The sky immediately changed color. GAME OVER appeared in letters of fire.

Liz had won. Raising her hands to her head, she pulled off the goggles, squeezing her eyes tightly shut for a moment before she opened them and looked toward Ariel.

The expression on the girl's face was savage and terrifying.

7

THERE WAS A STUNNED SILENCE in the dimly lit hall. Liz looked around, aware of the enormous number of people crowded around the arena, staring down at her and the defeated Ariel. Then BJ started clapping. Someone else took it up, and the sound swelled until it became thunderous applause.

Ariel slowly removed the headband and goggles and pulled off the gloves with her small white teeth. She ran her hand over her head, dragging her fingers through her long tail of hair. Sweat glistened on her high forehead. She slid off the table and, for a moment, it looked as if she was going to speak to Liz. Then she abruptly turned away and vanished into a darkened doorway.

The small, stout owner of the arcade came over to Liz, who was now sitting on the edge of the couch. He was struggling to conceal the mixture of surprise and anger on his face. He extended a surprisingly delicate hand and Liz grasped it. His grip was strong and firm.

"You're very good, very good indeed," he said quietly. "Ariel is—was—unbeaten on that machine."

"I guess I was just lucky," Liz said carefully, forcing herself to smile.

The man's smile was bitter. "I don't think so," he said, so softly that Liz wasn't sure if she had heard him. "I can offer you a job here. I'll set you up as the new champion, let them challenge you."

Liz shook her head. "I'm not sure I could repeat my performance."

The man smiled. "I watched you play. I saw you analyzing the game, working out the pattern and the spread of the meteors. You knew precisely when to jump and when to fire the stones at Ariel, knowing she'd have more than enough to look out for. I'm offering you a job."

"I don't want a job. Anyway, what about Ariel, what are you going to do to her—fire her?"

"Hardly. She's my daughter." The arcade owner turned to the audience and, with a great flourish, pulled a thick wad of plastic money out of an inside pocket. "Ladies and gentlemen, we have a new champion! And the Quayside Arcade is pleased to award one hundred credits to . . . to . . ." He turned to Liz: "I didn't get your name."

She thought furiously. "Halley," she said quickly.

"Halley?" he said, disbelief evident in his voice.

Liz looked him straight in the eye and nodded. "Halley."

* * *

"Halley?" BJ said as they left the arcade.

"What was I going to do?" she snapped. "Give him my real name?"

Her brother nodded. He could see the sense in that.

"It was the first name I could think of," she continued. "We were playing a game of meteors, so naturally I thought of comets . . . Halley's comet."

BJ patted his inside pocket. "So what are we going to do with all this cash?" he asked.

His sister snorted dismissively. "One hundred credits is not a lot of cash. We make ten times that amount every minute of every day."

"The only problem is that we don't have access to that money right now," BJ gently reminded her.

Liz nodded. "OK. So we need a place to rest, some food, and some equipment."

"And a corrupted copy of *Night's Castle*," her brother added.

"What then?"

BJ glanced in the dirty window of a shop selling out-of-date LCD flat-screen TVs. "One of us will have to play the game, go into it to see how it has been tampered with," he said softly, and then added in the same tone of voice: "Don't look around, but I think we're being followed."

"How many?" she asked, pausing to peer into a bookstore. Most of the books on display were the old CD format, but there were a few of the newer VR type, where the reader could participate in the novel.

"Six, I think. They look like some of the people from the arcade."

"Are you sure they're following us?" Liz asked. "And why?"

"I can think of one hundred reasons," he said with a grim smile.

Liz reached for her brother's hand and jerked him into an alley that ran down the side of a foul-smelling restaurant. Walking quickly, not daring to look back, they hurried past piles of garbage. Some of the heaped refuse shifted and parted, red-eyed children and adults staring at them as they darted past. The garbage shifted back into place, hiding the humans that lived in its midst.

The twins turned left at the bottom of the alley and then left again. BJ slowed down. "We're doubling back on ourselves."

Liz wasn't listening. She was looking over her shoulder. "They're still following us. What are we going to do?"

"Run," BJ shouted. His breath was coming in gasps, his goggles fogging up, making it difficult to see where he was going.

They set off at a run, following the narrow, filthy alleyway. Rats squealed as they raced past. But the rats didn't run; they stood their ground and stared at the fleeing humans. Some of them were as big as cats. The twins raced around a corner—into a dead end. They were turning back when the six youths who'd been following them ran into the alleyway, and immediately spread out to block their exit.

"We're in deep trouble," BJ gasped.

8

"WE WANT THE MONEY," one of the youths said, stepping forward. His breathing mask had been painted and shaped into a birdlike mask, long plastic feathers appearing like bushy eyebrows over the blue-lensed goggles. He was tall and skinny, dressed in a tight-fitting plastic one-piece suit that had been fashionable about five years previously. He was bald except for a long, thin band of hair down the middle of his head. The hair had been teased into spikes, but most of these were now lying limp and flat across his skull. He shoved out a gloved hand, fingers opening and closing. "We want the money," he repeated.

There were four young men and two women in the group. BJ concentrated on the one who had spoken and who was obviously the leader. The youth was twitching nervously, eyes blinking constantly behind his goggles, and he kept shifting from foot to foot.

"Burnouts," Liz said, guessing what he was thinking.

Her brother nodded. These were game addicts. Too many hours spent playing cheap high-speed VR games had affected their nervous systems, leaving them highly unstable and excitable.

"Money," the leader snarled, stepping forward. He

shook his right arm, which he held close to his side. A length of black chain slid into his hand.

"Give him the money," Liz muttered.

BJ shook his head stubbornly. "No. You won it for us; I'm not just going to give it away."

"I can win more," Liz hissed. "You won't be doing anything else if he hits you with that chain. And there are six of them, remember," she added.

BJ smiled tightly. "But it's like a game, Liz. If you can take out the leader, the rest of the pack will scatter."

"This isn't a game," his twin said earnestly.

"It is to them." BJ nodded at the approaching youth. "Look at him. He's spent so long in poorly programmed VR that his brain has been fried. He's grown accustomed to everything moving so quickly in games that this world must seem slow to him."

"Money!" The youth swung the chain in a tight arc, snapping it off the ground, striking sparks.

BJ stepped forward, gray eyes fixed on the young man. Although he was only five foot five, BJ's shoulders were broad and he exercised every day to keep fit. What most people took for fat was actually muscle. He knew that if he got hold of the young man he could disarm him.

"You're making a big mistake," the burnout whispered hoarsely, eyelids fluttering, feathers quivering. He kept rattling the chain, sending it slithering across the ground like a metallic snake. Behind him, the gang began cheering, settling down to watch the fight.

Liz backed up against the alley wall, eyes frantically searching the trash for a weapon she could use. But none of the discarded plastic and polystyrene was heavy enough to throw. She stopped. There was a dead rat at her feet. It was one of the new breeds, as big as a cat, with rows of needle-pointed teeth, glossy black fur tipped with red, and a finger-thick tail that was almost twice the length of the body. These rats were immune to most poisons, and she'd read recently that there were now ten times more than the number of humans living in the city. Some day they'd take over. She looked up at BJ again. The burnout was closing in with quick, jerky steps, the chain now buzzing in the air before him. Taking a deep breath, trying not to think about what she was doing, Liz reached down and grabbed the rat's tail.

BJ dodged the first snap of the chain. It sparked off the wall behind him in a cloud of dust. He tried to step in closer to the burnout, inside the swing of the chain, but the youth was fast, very fast. He hopped back out of the way in a sudden movement, the chain buzzing in the air before him. BJ felt it part the air in front of his face.

"It would have been easier to give me the money," the youth snarled.

"I suppose it's too late to change my mind?" BJ asked.

"Much too late." The burnout stretched out his left arm, shook it, and a second chain slid into his hand. With quick, practiced flicks of his wrist, he set the chains buzzing on either side of him like propellers. Then, slowly, very slowly, he brought them around until they were whirling before him in a protective shield. He stepped forward.

BJ took a step back. There was no way he could get through the lethal spinning chains. Maybe he could throw himself to one side.

Cold, gritty brick pushed against his back.

The burnout laughed. "Got your back to the wall, eh?" He moved closer.

The youth's senses, trained and tuned in the lightning-fast VR world, caught the flicker of movement to his right. He turned . . . just as the rat came flying out of the air, straight for his face, jaws gaping, claws outstretched. He screamed in absolute terror as the rat fell on his chest. The spinning chains lost their rhythm and twisted into a tight knotted tangle, wrapping themselves around his body, driving him to the ground.

Liz grabbed BJ's hand and pulled him away from the wall. They ran straight into the rest of the gang, staring at their leader, who was now rolling around on the ground, still entangled in the chains. One burnout stepped into their path, but BJ hit him hard with his shoulder as he ran past, sending him spinning back into a pile of garbage. The twins raced out of the alley—and stopped.

There was a slim hooded figure standing before them, directly in the center of the path. Without a word, the figure lifted an arm, and a wide-mouthed silver pistol gleamed in the dull light. There was a muted crack, and a blue-white spark shot from the pistol . . .

9

THE SPARK HISSED BETWEEN THE TWINS and exploded behind them into the heaped garbage, which immediately burst into flame. The hooded figure fired again, igniting the trash piled high against the opposite wall, creating a barrier of fire across the mouth of the alley. Dozens of the enormous rats scattered squealing from the flames.

The figure slipped the gun into the folds of the heavy cloak and pushed back the deep hood. It was Ariel, the small, thin, black-eyed girl from the Gaming Arcade. She was wearing a completely transparent full-face mask.

"A lot of people watched you win that money in the arcade," she said suddenly. Her voice was barely above a whisper and slightly rasping as if her throat had once been damaged. Without saying another word she turned away, leaving the twins looking at one another.

"What are we going to do?" BJ asked.

Liz glanced over her shoulder. The fire was beginning to go down, and they could hear shouts and screams of the burnouts in the alleyway beyond. Without saying a word, she caught her brother's hand and they both ran after the girl, just disappearing around a corner.

Ariel led them through a maze of side streets and alleyways. Although she didn't run, she seemed to move unnaturally fast, and the twins were soon panting, too breathless to ask any questions even if they had been able to catch up with the girl. She stopped only once, when a pack of wild dogs tumbled out of a derelict building directly in front of them. Snapping and snarling, they dropped their bellies to the ground and crept toward the trio. Ariel produced the silver pistol and pointed it at the largest dog. It immediately stopped, recognizing the danger. For a long moment the savage dog and the black-eyed girl stared at one another. Then the dog turned and vanished into the shadows, followed by the rest of the pack.

Ariel finally led them to the towering graffiti-daubed walls of the very edge of the Quays. The enormous, ancient walls, with their massive square bricks, had once enclosed the river that flowed through the city. Dozens of ramshackle buildings had been constructed against them, rickety structures of plastic and hardboard, thick cardboard, lengths of cloth, and twisted scraps of metal. In places, whole sections of the wall had been hacked out into shallow openings to provide a home for entire families. Steep and narrow stairways had been set onto the side of the wall, leading upward into the gloom. Without pausing, the silent girl darted up the stairs.

The twins stopped at the bottom of the stairs, panting with exertion. "Why are we following her?" BJ asked.

"Because we've got nowhere else to go. And she did save our lives," Liz reminded him.

BJ straightened. He looked at the stairs and smiled at his sister. "Ladies first."

There were one hundred and fifteen steps—Liz counted every one—and each step was barely wide enough for one person to walk on. There was no railing, only a sheer drop to the dirty streets below.

As they climbed, they discovered more openings in the walls, artificial caves created around unused drainage pipes and sewers. Sheets of plastic and old rags hung across the entrances, but the twins saw the families crouched in the gloom. Usually only their eyes, wide and staring, gave away their numbers. Among the few scraps of furniture, there was nearly always a TV or a gaming machine shedding its flickering light, making shadows dance up the damp walls.

The steps stopped in a dead end.

Ariel was sitting on the topmost step, her legs dangling out over the void, when the twins finally panted up. They crouched behind her, their backs firmly to the wall.

"Now what?" Liz asked.

"We wait," Ariel whispered.

Liz suddenly squeezed her brother's arm and pointed with a trembling finger at the back of the girl's neck. BJ squinted, seeing nothing. Then he noticed that the girl's long mane of hair had shifted in the stale breeze, revealing a small metallic plug inserted into the flesh at the base of her skull. It was a standard computer jack.

Ariel turned around suddenly. The girl's hard black eyes were like marbles; it was impossible to read any expression in them. "My father wants to talk to you."

"The arcade owner?" Liz asked. "But I already told him

I wasn't interested in his offer."

Ariel ignored her. She looked up as a swaying rope ladder appeared out of an opening in the shadows above and dropped down.

BJ stared up. "We don't have to climb that, do we?"

Without a word, Ariel stood and pulled herself up the ladder.

BJ looked at his sister. "We can go up . . . or down," he said. They both leaned forward to look down onto the Quays far below. "We go up," they said together.

It was sixty rungs to the top of the ladder. Liz went first and climbed laboriously to the top, collapsing when she got there. Even before he was halfway up, BJ could feel the muscles in his back and shoulders beginning to protest. Although he was fit and strong, he was now hauling his entire weight upward. By the fortieth rung, he felt as if his back were on fire. By the fiftieth, he could no longer feel his hands, which were tingling with pins and needles. He stopped, five rungs from the top.

Liz, now partly recovered, leaned out over the edge. "Come on, BJ. You're nearly there."

There was a tight band across his chest, making every breath agony. His neck and shoulder muscles were knotted balls of fire and his fingers felt swollen. "I can't," he managed to whisper. "I'm not going to make it. I'm going to fall," he added, his voice shaking.

Ariel caught Liz's shoulder and pulled her back. "Hold my legs," she rasped. Lying flat on the ground, she waited until Liz had caught hold of her legs, then she reached down for the top rung and hauled it upward. The muscles in her shoulders and arms stood out as she stretched down to catch the next rung.

"I can't hold on!" BJ shouted.

"Hold on," Ariel snapped. She pulled the next two rungs up quickly. But the shuddering vibrations shook the boy's grasp loose. One hand came free . . . and Ariel's iron-fingered grip closed around his wrist. With a muscle-cracking effort, she hauled him up by the arm, caught his shoulder, and almost threw him back on top of Liz.

Ariel stood, swinging her arms and working her shoulders. BJ started to thank her, but she brushed past him, stepping into a low, narrow tunnel set into the wall.

Footsteps approached, echoing off the metal walls and floor of the tunnel.

"Welcome," a voice boomed out of the shadows. "Welcome. You're perfectly safe here. There's only one entrance, and you have seen how difficult it is to get in that way. And even if anyone did succeed in getting that far, we have a few other surprises for them!" The small, stout figure of the arcade owner loomed up out of the darkness. "Just as you have a few surprises in store for us, eh?"

He crouched down in front of the twins, and his daughter stood behind him, one hand on his shoulder. He was staring intently at them both. "I watched you play," he said to Liz. "I've seen the top VR players in the world. I've watched my daughter day after day. I've seen her become an expert. And then I've taken those learned skills and added them to the program, making it better . . . forcing her to become better. Ariel should be unbeatable. But you beat her. I finally realized that only one type of person could have beaten Ariel—a Game Master, or perhaps a Game Maker." He smiled quickly, showing perfect teeth. "Once I realized that, the rest was easy. You're BJ and Liz O'Connor, owners of Gemini Corporation, one of the most profitable companies in the Free World. You've been called the finest Game Makers since Aaron Harper." The man's smile grew broader. "Well, we'll see if you deserve that reputation."

"I don't know what you're talking about," BJ muttered.

"I am Aaron Harper," the stout man said.

Liz shook her head. "Harper is dead."

The man considered for a moment, then nodded slightly. "Living in this place, I might as well be." He stood up and dusted off his knees. "But come, come. You and I can be useful to one another."

"I'm not sure how," Liz said cautiously.

"It's all over the news. You created an illegal game. Police have orders to shoot you on sight." He stood back, allowing them to precede him down the metal tube—it had once been a sewer—into a large circular room.

"First we'll eat," Harper said, following them into the room, "then you can tell me how you got into this mess."

10

"WE BELIEVE THEY'RE ON THE QUAYS," Captain Lyons said to the flat screen set into the wall above his desk. The screen was blank, but Lyons knew that somewhere deep in the building the enormous mainframe computer was recording his every word and making decisions based upon the data. "The twins have effectively vanished from the city. Although they are on the most wanted list, there have been no sightings, they have not used their credit cards, nor have they contacted any of their friends or colleagues. Therefore, it seems logical to assume that they have gone into the Quays, where we are unable to track them."

"Your assumptions would seem to be correct."

Although the voice was female, Lyons knew it was a computer-generated sound. He thought it sounded sharp and false; he preferred the old artificial machine voice it had replaced.

"This conclusion confirms my opinion that the twins were creating illegal games and selling them throughout the Quays. We know there is a trade in highly violent and X-rated games in the arcades on the Quays. It is my opinion that the game now under investigation, *Night's*

Castle, was one of these games, and that it accidentally slipped onto the general market."

"Night's Castle *is neither excessively violent nor does it carry an X-certificate. There is no evidence that Gemini Corporation has been involved in the creation of illegal or prohibited games,"* the computer voice said.

"We have a dozen people in the hospital, locked in a VR coma. They were all playing *Night's Castle* when the attack occurred."

"That would suggest that one or more copies of the game are defective. There is no evidence that Gemini Corporation manufactured it in that condition."

Lyons took a deep breath. He believed the greatest mistake the police department had ever made was putting in these super-computers, "thinking machines" they had been called. They were ideal for solving simple cases, where the machines could access the vast network of computer data. But police work was more than just collecting data. It was instinct, too. And, right now, his every instinct was telling him that the twins were involved in something big. If he could prove it, it would make his reputation and guarantee him a promotion. And it would settle a very old score.

"I would like permission to send undercover officers into the Quays to look for the twins."

"Permission granted for a maximum of three officers to go undercover into the Quays. A list of suitable officers is being sent to your console now."

Lyons was careful to keep his face expressionless. He knew he was being taped and that the tape would be used when the case went to court.

"I would also like the citywide computer network monitored for any unauthorized entry or use of power."

"Explain, please."

"I believe the twins may try to access the computer network to destroy incriminating records in their own computer system or possibly to transfer funds from their accounts to another account."

"That course of action has now been initiated. All attempted entry into the data network will be traced back to its source."

"This concludes my report," Captain Lyons said, turning away.

"Report filed," the blank screen said.

When the captain sat down at his desk, he pulled up the flat plastic screen and touched the keypad. A dozen names, ranks, and skills appeared in warm orange letters. Without looking, he picked two at random. He knew he had permission for three officers: he intended to be the third. He would bring the twins to justice personally.

11

ARIEL DROPPED TWO PLATES onto the large round table that took up the center of the high circular room. Blobs of thick gray liquid spatted across their scarred surfaces. BJ and Liz sat in wire-mesh seats and looked at the lumpy porridge.

"I know what it looks like," Aaron Harper said with a smile, sinking into a creaking metal chair, "so just close your eyes and eat it. It will taste like chicken casserole."

BJ moved the thick gooey substance around the plate, staring at it suspiciously. It looked revolting, but the smell made his mouth water and his stomach gurgled. It had been a long time since breakfast. Scooping up a gray glob, he sniffed it. It smelled like chicken, and he knew it would probably taste like chicken though it looked like something you'd find in a clogged waste pipe. The twins were wealthy enough to be able to afford real food, but he'd almost forgotten that the vast majority of people ate refined and textured soya and tofu, fortified with vitamins and minerals.

BJ glanced at his sister. She was spooning the disgusting mess into her mouth, her eyes tightly closed. Following her example, BJ squeezed his eyes shut, opened his mouth, and took a spoonful of the soya. It tasted a lot better than it looked.

"You get used to it," the small, stout man said as they ate. "Real food—real meat, real fruit, real vegetables—is a luxury of the very wealthy. It's hard to believe that less than one hundred years ago there was actually a food surplus in the world."

"What happened?" Liz asked, swallowing hard. Although the food tasted fine, it *felt* disgusting in her mouth.

"Depletion of the ozone layer led to a gradual buildup of radiation in the soil. When the weather systems began to change in the late 1990s, bringing a combination of flooding and drought, much of the world's food-growing capacity was effectively halved and halved again as the greenhouse effect took control. By the early 2020s, all food was grown under glass." He nodded at their plates. "Much of this muck is now grown underground in the vast caverns beneath the Sahara Desert or under the domes on the dark side of the moon."

BJ pushed away his half-empty plate. He could feel the jellylike mass sitting in the pit of his stomach. It moved when he did.

"Here . . ." Harper slid two fat plastic tubes bearing the cola company symbol across the table. *Now with Real Sugar* was printed along the side. "This will take the taste away." The twins snapped the tops off the tubes and sucked at the thin brown liquid, washing the greasy soya off their tongues.

"When we get this mess sorted out, Mr. Harper," Liz said quickly, "we'll pay you back."

Harper smiled quickly, but the smile never touched his eyes. "There'll be time enough to talk of payment later. First we have to decide what we're going to do with you." He glanced at the watch on his wrist, then turned to the curved metal wall behind him. "Viewer," he said clearly.

A flat screen, less than an inch thick, dropped into place.

"Channel Four," Harper said.

The screen flickered, distortion flowing down its LCD screen in long vivid waves before it settled. The Channel Four news logo flashed up onto the screen and a deep voice announced, *"News every hour on the hour."*

A young woman appeared on the screen. Her smile never wavered as she spoke quickly of food riots in Central Europe, a citywide fire in one of the American super-cities, and the discovery of another hole—the twenty-second—in the ozone layer directly above the city of Paris. Each item was accompanied by fifteen seconds of film. Finally Gemini Corporation's logo flashed up onto the screen, followed by images of the twins.

"In a shock move today, police raided the luxury apartments of BJ and Liz O'Connor, the youthful directors of Gemini Corporation." The next image showed a hospital ward. Banks of monitoring equipment lined the walls, attached to the still bodies in the beds by lines of multicolored tubing. *"This hospital ward now holds twelve people in VR coma. All the victims were playing* Night's Castle, *the best-selling VR game from Gemini Corporation."* An image of the Night's Castle logo flashed

65

up on the screen. *"Police suspect that the multi-millionaire Game Makers have developed an illegal game, and all copies of* Night's Castle *have been withdrawn. Purchasers are requested to return their copies of the game and to see their doctors immediately. The O'Connors were unavailable for comment, and rumors coming out of the police department would seem to indicate that they have fled the country. And now over to the weather department . . ."*

"Off," Harper snapped. The image died and the screen retreated up into the ceiling. The stout man turned to face the twins, his fingers locked together as if for prayer. Ariel stood behind him, her coal-black eyes looking like holes in her unnaturally white face. She rested a long-fingered hand on her father's shoulder and stared at Liz.

"You two are in a lot of trouble," Harper said.

BJ slammed his fist onto the metal table. "*Night's Castle* was safe! I wrote the code, checked it, checked it again and again before we even created a rough working model of the VR world. Then both Liz and I played the game for months, developing, altering, and refining the game before we thought about releasing it to the public."

"It was also passed by the Board of Game Control," Liz added. "They gave it a general certificate."

"But there are people in a VR coma," Aaron Harper said simply. "And the only connection is your game." He jerked his thumb at the wall where the screen had been. "On an earlier bulletin, it said that one of the victims is a VR police officer who was actually playing the game when he went unconscious."

"The game was safe," BJ repeated stubbornly.

"Therefore the structure of the game has been altered," Liz said slowly. "But how? It would take great skill to alter the internal structure of the game, and very few people would have access to the hardware required. And why?" she wondered.

The arcade owner spread his hands wide. "To ruin you, of course." He saw the twins' blank looks. "You are wealthy, very, very wealthy. Great wealth attracts envy and envy is a dangerous emotion. Who would hate you badly enough to ruin you?"

The twins looked at one another, shaking their heads at the same time. "I suppose Captain Lyons in Department 13 is the closest we have to an enemy," Liz said eventually. "But he's more of a nuisance than anything else."

"Would your parents have had any enemies?" Harper asked quickly.

"Our parents were lost when that comet hit the moon eight years ago," BJ said quickly. "We took over Gemini Corporation when they died. If they had any enemies, we never met them."

Something flickered across Harper's face. Liz leaned across the table. "But you knew all this, didn't you?"

Harper smiled. "You are quick . . . very quick." He nodded slightly. "I knew your parents. I even worked with them briefly."

The arcade owner leaned back in the creaking chair and looked up at the rusting metal ceiling. There was an almost sad smile on his thin lips. "I was a Game Maker once, like you, though never as good. But in my day I was considered brilliant. When your parents were experimenting with organic memory, storing data in simple animal and plant tissue, I created the first ever computer-human link. All of today's VR software is made possible because of my breakthrough. In my day, I had a nickname . . ."

"The Harper," BJ breathed. "You were a famous Game Maker in your time, but your reputation was destroyed when you were accused of making an illegal game that caused thousands of deaths before the link with the game was discovered. Directly after that, Department 13, the VR police, was set up."

Harper slapped both hands down on the metal table, the sound like a gunshot in the metal room. "I was framed, destroyed by those who were jealous of my achievement and success." He took a deep breath, calming himself. "And I won't sit by and see it happen to you. Your parents were good to me, they stood by me when everyone else doubted me. The moment I saw you playing in the arcade, I knew you were no ordinary VR player. When I looked at you closely," he said to Liz, "I could see your mother's features. She was very beautiful." He added, "And then when I heard the news and realized what had happened, I knew I had to help you. Your parents were my very good friends. So you could say I'm repaying an old debt."

"I always thought The Harper was dead," BJ whispered.

The stout man spread his arms wide, taking in the room and the murky world outside. "Would you call this living?" he asked.

12

THE ROOM WAS LONG AND NARROW, made even more cramped by the computer banks covering three of the four walls. There were cables everywhere, dripping from the ceiling, snaking across the floor, curling from the walls in thick multicolored loops. Four enormous flat screens took up the remaining wall. Three were dark, while one flickered and shuddered with multicolored interference that pulsed in time to the low, insistent hum that vibrated through the room.

Aaron Harper strode into the center of the room. "Welcome to my kingdom," he announced.

The twins stood in the doorway, looking at the tangled maze of equipment, a mixture of old and new, some of it so outdated that it was almost antique, sitting alongside the latest equipment of the type they used themselves.

"Where do you get your power?" Liz wondered, looking at the rat's nest of wires and cables, realizing that it would need an immense amount of power to run it. "Surely the Central Grid doesn't supply you?"

Harper grinned hugely. "Not knowingly. But don't forget, I was once one of the foremost programmers in the world. What would you do in my situation?"

"Tap into the central power grid," Liz said immediately.

BJ grinned. "Free power."

The man nodded. "That's exactly what I do. I take a tiny percentage of power from a hundred different industrial complexes all across the city. They never even miss it."

"What do you do with all this stuff?" BJ asked, stepping into the room, looking around at the equipment, ancient flat keyboards, slender microprocessors, glass boxes holding the organic memory modules that their parents—and Harper too—had developed. He picked up an old-fashioned CD, turning it around in his hands. "I didn't know they were still making these."

"They're not," Harper said, lifting the disc out of his hands. "That disc is eighty years old."

"Why do you still need it?" BJ continued. "What do you use it for?"

Liz stood back and watched Harper and her brother. She knew what her twin was doing. He was distracting Harper, giving her time to look around and evaluate the extraordinary equipment. Much of it was for game-making—virtual reality image processors, compilers, programming tools. Harper was still developing games, but were they only for his own arcade, or did he sell them on the open market too? If he lived on the Quays, he could be selling only into the illegal market. She found herself wondering exactly what type of games the old Game Maker created. She caught a glimpse of a reflection in the monitor before her and turned, discovering Ariel staring unblinkingly at her.

Liz deliberately turned away, finding the smaller girl's

hard stare unnerving. "You still haven't told us what you do," she said to Harper.

The round-faced man blinked in surprise. "Haven't I? Why, I would have thought it was obvious. I develop computer software."

"Games?" BJ asked quickly, glancing at his sister.

Harper nodded slowly. "Some games, yes. A lot of the games in the arcade are mine, though the players don't know that. That's why I was so surprised when you beat Ariel. She and I developed that game together; none knows it better than she."

"Where do you sell your work?" Liz asked quietly. She ran her hand across her close-cropped hair, feeling it buzz and crackle beneath her fingers with all the static electricity in the air.

"Wherever I can," Harper said easily. His thin lips curled in a smile. "I sell into the Far East, and the Unified States are still a big market." His smile faded. "Officially, of course, I'm not allowed to develop anything. I was sentenced to five years in a VR prison." He shuddered. "You cannot imagine what that's like. My mind knew I was lying asleep in a hospital bed, but my body thought I was in a prison on an island in the middle of the Atlantic. What's terrifying about VR prison is that your own fears make it worse. When I came out of prison, I was banned from developing software for life." He shrugged. "But what was I supposed to do? I'm trained for nothing else; I can do nothing else. So I went underground—or rather I came down onto the Quays and disappeared. I continued working. It hasn't been easy. It was always a struggle to get the latest equipment, then power, then the software.

The software, especially the latest games, were always the most difficult to find. However," he smiled again, "I succeeded. Show them, Ariel."

The twins looked at the girl, but she simply turned away and disappeared between two tall processing units.

"Go with her," Harper said.

Liz turned sideways and slid through the opening into a second room. It was long, narrow, and high. Its metal walls were covered with thin metal shelves, all of them filled with brightly colored plastic packages.

"This is my father's software library," Ariel said in her rasping whisper. "Here you will find every important piece of software that has been released in the past ten years." Her face moved in what might have been a smile. "Including every game issued by Gemini Corporation."

"Why does your father collect these games?" Liz asked.

"Do you not collect your competitors' games?" Ariel asked sharply. "Don't you watch to see what they're doing?" she demanded.

Liz nodded.

BJ trailed his fingers along the edges of the shelves. "I know a lot of these," he said quietly, his voice echoing off the metal floor and high ceiling, "though there are some I've never seen before." He lifted one and handed it to his sister.

Liz turned the package over, looking at the badly printed cover of a warrior holding a blazing pistol. *The Annihilator. You can kill your enemies with any one of a dozen weapons,* she read. *Accepts 2D photographs and 3D holograms of all your enemies and incorporates them into the game. Watch them die . . .* The girl turned the box over again, looking for a recommended age group or a Department 13 sticker. There was none. "This game wasn't passed by the censors," she remarked. "It's a banned game."

"It's banned here in this country, though it's available if you know where to look. In the Far East it sold close to two million copies," Ariel said proudly.

From the tone of her voice, Liz guessed that the game had been written by Harper.

"It's not different from any of the games you've written."

"We don't chop up or burn or stab or shoot people in our games," Liz said quickly. "We don't put the faces of real people on our characters."

Again the quick, jerky movement of Ariel's face that passed for a smile. "In *Night's Castle*, the vampires are stabbed and chopped up . . ."

"But that's fantasy," BJ said.

"So is this." Ariel defended her father's work. She turned and reached up onto the shelf behind her, pulling out a copy of *Night's Castle.* Then, without another word, she brushed past the twins and stepped back into the outer room.

"I've got a feeling we were safer out on the Quays," BJ whispered, as they followed the girl.

✽   ✽   ✽

They were sitting around the circular table in the outer room, the copy of *Night's Castle* in the center of the table.

"You know you will have to go into the game?" Harper said slowly, his delicate fingers touching the plastic box, turning it around. "You will have to play it through to try to discover the programming errors."

73

"There are no errors," Liz said quietly.

"But there is something wrong; you do admit that?"

The twins nodded.

"And if you go into the game," Harper continued, "you do realize the risk you're taking?"

BJ smiled. "We know this game better than anyone. We made it; it is our world."

The Harper's smile was cold. "Let us assume for the moment that your programming was correct: why then is your game sending people into a VR coma?" He looked at BJ and Liz and hurried on before either of them could answer. "Because this *isn't* the game you created. Someone has interfered with it, altered it."

"A virus," BJ whispered.

Aaron Harper nodded. "Very probably."

"And if we go into the game," Liz said slowly, "then that same virus will attack us."

"It will," Harper agreed. "However, you have an advantage over those others who played the game and fell victim to the virus: you are the game's creators. You know this world inside out. The moment there is something amiss you will know it. There's even a chance that you might be able to defeat it."

"The word I don't like is 'might,'" BJ said grimly. "What happens if we don't defeat it and the virus overpowers us?"

"Then you too will fall into a VR coma," the small man said simply.

Liz reached over and lifted the box, looking at the 3D image of a crumbling castle highlighted by a full moon. Tiny bats flitted across the face of the moon. She looked at Harper. "Do we have a choice?" she asked.

Harper spread his hands and shrugged his shoulders. "Of course you have a choice. You don't have to take the risk. But if you don't clear your name you will end up in prison or living as a fugitive like me."

Liz turned to look at her twin. Even before she asked him, she knew what his answer would be.

"We don't have a choice!" he said simply.

13

SITTING IN THE LONG, NARROW ROOM before the flat screen, his fingers moving swiftly across the old-fashioned keyboard, Aaron Harper called up the camera monitoring the twins' room. They were both asleep, lying on narrow metal cots in a low-ceilinged circular room. Ariel's long, delicate fingers tuned in the sensors that monitored the twins' heart, respiration, and brain waves. Data began scrolling down two separate screens too fast to read.

"I will analyze the data later," Harper murmured. He looked at his daughter. "What do you think?"

"I don't know about the boy but the girl is fast—very fast," Ariel whispered. "I could have defeated her," she added immediately.

"I know that," Harper said quickly. He nodded toward the screen. "But it was important that she was allowed to win. We needed to bring them here. We need them to trust us—for the moment. Tomorrow, they will go into their own VR world of *Night's Castle*. I will monitor the game from here." He paused and then added softly. "I know it is dangerous, but I want you to go with them."

"Why?" Ariel demanded. Her black eyes were reflecting the data scrolling down the screens, recording the twins' dreams. She was astonished to discover that the two screens—BJ's and Liz's—were identical.

"Watch them, learn from them. We must learn everything we can from them, it's our one chance . . . but we must protect them too. We owe them that much."

Ariel turned away, shaking her head. "We don't owe them anything," she snapped.

✳   ✳   ✳

Captain Lyons was just leaving the police cruiser when the call came in. His name and rank blinked on the screen in bright yellow letters; the yellow color indicated that this was a personal call. He pressed RECEIVE, but surprisingly nothing happened. The screen didn't clear to reveal the face of the person calling him. While he was fiddling with the controls, the tiny speaker crackled. *"The O'Connor twins will enter the VR world of* Night's Castle *at precisely noon tomorrow."*

14

"I WILL BE ABLE TO CONTROL THE GAME from here," Aaron Harper said pointing to the four wall screens. Ariel stood by his side, with her back to the screens, watching the twins. "If I notice anything unusual, I'll be able to pull you out of there."

"No," Liz said immediately. "It's the unusual we're looking for. If you pull us out just as something starts to happen, we'll probably never discover what's gone wrong with the game."

"As you wish," Harper said. "But what will you do if you encounter something unusual?"

BJ lifted his left arm. A thin metal sleeve covered his arm from wrist to elbow. It was studded with tiny buttons and winking lights. "This is a microcomputer programmed with all our programming data. Before we go into the VR world, we'll hook it up to your mainframe. If anything happens in the VR world, it will show up here and then I'll be able to alter the programming from within the game."

"Ingenious," Harper breathed. "And, of course, the obvious next step in game-making. Programming the game from within!"

"I invented it myself," BJ said proudly.

Harper's eyes lingered on the metal sleeve, until his daughter touched his arm. "Tell them," she whispered.

"Tell us what?" Liz asked.

Harper smiled. "Ariel will accompany you into your VR world."

The twins shook their heads simultaneously. "It's too risky. Too dangerous," Liz said.

"You don't understand," Harper continued. "My daughter has been involved in the creation of software since she was a child. Her knowledge of computer systems and viruses is second to none. If she is with you, she should be able to recognize the virus that is infecting your game." He paused and added softly, "And she has one great advantage . . ."

Ariel turned around. Placing both hands on the back of her head, she lifted up her long tail of jet-black hair to reveal the circular stud at the base of her skull.

"When I worked with your parents, we realized very early on that the human brain is perfectly capable of processing the vast amounts of data that a computer generates." Harper reached forward and tapped a screen. "The data is displayed on a screen, but the problem, of course, is that the human eye is not capable of taking it all in. So we devised a way of bypassing the optic nerve. Ariel can now receive computer input direct from the machine into her brain, where it is instantly sorted and processed. In this way she can 'learn' in minutes what would normally take years to acquire."

Ariel dropped her hair back in place and turned around. "The human brain uses only a tiny percentage of its capacity," she whispered. "My father created a process that enables me to access much more of the brain's potential. Once this process is perfected, everyone can become a genius: the sum total of the world's knowledge can be programmed into the human brain in seconds."

Harper nodded. "Years ago, I created the first truly successful human-computer link in the form of the VR goggles and gloves you wear today." He touched the back of Ariel's neck. "This is the next step: the ability to plug directly into the machine. To become part of the machine!"

Liz nodded doubtfully. "I can see that it has enormous potential. But I don't see how it can help us."

"Once she becomes part of the machine, once she enters the machine world, Ariel becomes as fast, as smart as the machine. In the VR world, she is superhuman, she is a god, with all the powers of a god."

"But if you're that powerful," BJ said, "why can't you destroy the virus now?"

"At the moment, I cannot distinguish between what is part of the game program and what is virused. Your own security and anti-tampering codes prevent me from gaining access to parts of the program. Teach me the difference and I can then immediately destroy the virused portions of your game."

Harper added, "Now you see why she has to go with you."

BJ and Liz looked at one another and nodded.

*　　*　　*

The twins lay on long, narrow metal cots in Harper's control room. Ariel sat at a console with a thin red wire disappearing into her hair at the back of her neck. Data flashed down the screens too fast to read, and though the girl's eyes were closed, she seemed to be following it, her head moving and twitching as the screens changed.

Harper handed the twins their VR goggles and gloves and a small jar of petroleum jelly. Dipping their fingers into the jar, they smeared the jelly onto their temples and fingertips to ensure a good connection between the skin and the VR equipment.

BJ slipped a flat plug into his metal sleeve and pressed the ON switch. Red, green, and white lights flowed across the sleeve in a quick sequence. "All set," he said, looking sidelong at his sister. She nodded quickly. The twins pulled on the skintight gloves and settled the narrow goggles over their eyes.

Flickering gray lines buzzed across their retinas.

They could hear Harper's voice in the background. "I'll watch you from here. If you get into any trouble that you can't handle, I'll do the best I can to help you. When the game is running you can talk to me, but I cannot talk to you . . . so you really are on your own."

"We know that," Liz said.

"You can still call this off."

"If we don't do this, we'll be hunted as criminals for the rest of our lives," BJ said.

"As you wish." Keys clicked. "I'm beginning the pre-game sequence now."

The twins watched as the flickering lines of interference vanished and the world changed to a dull gray light. In the top right-hand corner of the sky, a tiny clock appeared with the seconds slowly ticking away.

11:59:30

Harper's voice boomed around them, the last time before the game began that they would be able to hear him. "I'll allow you to remain in the game for an hour. Then I'll save it and pull you out."

11:59:45

"The best of luck!"

At precisely twelve o'clock, BJ and Liz, accompanied by Ariel, entered the VR world of *Night's Castle*.

❋   ❋   ❋

On the other side of the city, Captain Eddie Lyons was watching an enormous grid map of the city and the Quays. Lights flowed and flickered across the map, indicating computer usage. Bright lights showed where major corporations and offices were using their machines, small winking ones where personal users were working on their machines at home.

At precisely twelve noon, Lyons said: "Concentrate on the Quays."

The screen flickered and changed, the majority of lights disappearing dramatically. There were four major uses of computer power in the Quays.

"Identify the sources."

"Three are legitimate games arcades," the female computer voice said. *"The fourth is unrecognized and unauthorized."*

Lyons grinned triumphantly. He had them now!

15

BJ AND LIZ WERE STANDING on a barren, rocky plain beneath a sky the color of metal. Gray-black clouds massed on the horizon. Faint, very faint, but growing louder, an organ began the *Night's Castle* theme, the sound carried on the wind. The music swelled to a crescendo, the ground trembling in time to the rhythm, the vibrations knocking the twins off their feet. And then, directly in front of them, the earth ruptured and the Gemini Corporation logo, in shimmering silver metal, rose out of the ground.

Thunder rumbled, lightning flashed, and then: WELCOME . . . TO *NIGHT'S CASTLE* beamed across the sky. Flashing streaks of jagged lightning spelled out *NIGHT'S CASTLE* in letters forty feet high.

BJ got to his feet. "I really like that bit."

"Only because it's your voice." Liz grinned, steadying herself.

BJ lifted his left arm and looked at his metal sleeve. The colored lights were moving smoothly across the band. He raised his head and spoke to the sky. "Harper, if you're receiving clear pictures and sound, give us a signal."

On the four large screens in the control room, Aaron Harper watched the twins from different angles. His fingers moved a tiny black joystick.

Colors flooded the gray sky, red, green, blue, yellow, and gold appearing in smooth swirls.

BJ grinned. "I take it you're receiving us." He touched his sleeve. "Now, I just want to make sure I'm in control." He tapped in a brief control sequence.

The clouds disappeared, leaving a checkerboard sky of black and white squares.

"Stop it," Liz snapped, "you're making me dizzy."

BJ brought back the clouds. "I was just checking," he said. He looked around. "Where's Ariel? I thought she was coming in with us?"

Liz turned to examine the rocky landscape. "So did I," she murmured.

"Maybe she changed her mind at the last minute." BJ rubbed his hands briskly together. "Well, the game looks the same," he said.

Liz knelt down and scooped up a handful of gray grit. The real secret of the twins' success as Game Makers was the detail they put into the game. Although Liz *knew* that she was lying on a bed in Harper's control room, the incredibly detailed images her brain was receiving made it easy to believe that she was standing on a barren ledge holding a handful of grit. She could actually feel the texture of the sandy pebbles beneath her fingers. As she watched, a tiny insect crawled out of the grit and dropped from her hand onto the ground.

"The detail is still good," she said, brushing her hands together. Usually when a game went bad or when a virus attacked the computer memory, it was the small details that disappeared first—the texture of the stones, the scent of the grass, the reflected colors on the surface of water.

BJ examined the sky. In the distance, over a dark mountain range, a ragged streak of lightning crashed to earth. "And the timing is still in sync," he said. Another sure sign that a game was in trouble was when the sound and picture slipped ever so slightly out of synchronization, like a badly dubbed film where the actors' lips keep moving even though no one is speaking. "We'd better get moving," he continued. "It's going to rain right about . . . now!"

On cue the heavens opened and rain poured down over the twins. Pulling their coats over their heads, they ran for the shelter of a clump of tall standing stones. The raindrops were large and heavy, spattering off their plastic clothing, stinging where they touched flesh, splashing onto the ground, bouncing off the grit.

They raced into the shelter of the stones and shook the water off their clothes. "The rain was your idea," BJ said quickly.

"Tell me again why we made this world so uncomfortable?" Liz asked.

"Because you wanted to see if you could program raindrops," he reminded her. He lifted his left arm and touched his metal sleeve. "I can make it stop raining. I can take out the line in the program," he suggested.

"Don't you dare!" Liz snapped. "It took me two weeks just to get this sequence right."

BJ shrugged. Looking up into the sky, he said, "Time?"

12:04:32 appeared in the sky in bright red letters.

"It should stop raining in less than thirty seconds," he said, beginning to count backward.

But it didn't stop. It continued raining, pounding down in huge drops, churning the ground at their feet into thick mud, pooling in their boots, trickling down the back of their necks. Although it was only an illusion, it was as uncomfortable as the real thing. Thunder boomed close by; lightning flashed to the ground behind them. The air was suddenly filled with the odor of burnt metal. Liz felt the hair on her scalp itch with the electricity in the air.

This wasn't in the program!

Thunder rattled again, almost directly overhead. The stench of ozone was sickening.

Liz suddenly caught her brother and dragged him away from the rock, pulling him to the ground just as a lightning bolt exploded across the stone in a thunderous detonation, slicing it in half. Hot pebbles rained down on top of them. Scrambling to their feet, they raced away from the low hilltop, just as another dozen lightning bolts sliced down on it in quick succession, churning the stones and earth into a smoking ruin.

The rain ceased as suddenly as it had begun.

Liz stopped running and bent double, a pain in her side. Looking up into the sky, she called: "Isolate that last sequence, Harper. That definitely wasn't part of our programming."

Aaron Harper switched one of the screens to look at the scrolling lines of machine code that showed the game in progress. But at no point did it show a lightning attack on the players. Whatever virus was in the game was deeply hidden. He shook his head, puzzled.

"Time?" BJ panted.

12:05:55

"Less than eight minutes into the game and we've been attacked. God knows what's ahead of us."

The twins continued down the narrow track, BJ constantly monitoring the game on his metal sleeve, Liz watching the surroundings for anything out of the ordinary.

In virtual reality, the Game Makers had the chance to be god, to design whole worlds and everything in them. However, most Game Makers didn't bother that much. They created square fields for the game to take place in. It was possible for the player to walk right up to the edge of the field and see the rest of the world disappear into a gray nothingness. The difference with the twins' creations was that they created whole worlds, complete in every direction. In one of their games, players could walk for days and completely encircle the world, arriving right back where they had started off. Because the twins were programming on such a big scale, because their creations weren't cramped within a square mile, they were able to add incredible complexity to their games. One of the reasons Gemini Corporation's games were so successful was because the players got the impression that they were actually in a real world.

Liz usually enjoyed traveling through any of the VR worlds she and BJ had created. No matter how wild and bizarre it was—an alien landscape, a fantasy creation, a nightmare atmosphere—she always felt safe. This was their world. They had created it, like god creating the Garden of Eden.

They climbed up out of a small valley . . . and stopped. A deep gash cut through the landscape from north to south. A complex bridge of twisted ropes and vines had been strung across the chasm. It swayed gently in the breeze. The twins looked at one another: this wasn't part of their original program.

They might be gods in this Garden of Eden . . . but they were sharing it with a serpent.

16

THE TWINS STOOD AT THE EDGE of the chasm and looked down. The land disappeared into shadow a long way below. BJ moved closer to the edge, earth crumbling away from beneath his feet and spinning off into the pit. "I can program this out," he said quietly, lifting his arm.

Liz shook her head slightly. "If we start programming out the new bits, we might activate the virus and cause it to spread. We'll cross the bridge." Reaching over, she caught her brother's left arm, twisting it to look at the metal sleeve. Without saying a word, she tapped the console.

BJ looked at it, wondering what his sister saw . . . and then realized that the sequence of colored lights was still moving smoothly. The alarm light should be flashing, indicating that the game code had been interfered with. Either the computer didn't recognize the new additions to the game or it was defective. There was something wrong here!

"I'll go first," Liz interrupted. "You wait here until I've got across."

BJ nodded absently. His fingers moved across the keypad, testing various functions of the metal sleeve. They all checked out. He looked at the chasm again and had a sudden, terrifying thought: if his machine didn't recognize the new portions of the game, would it be able to act upon them? He was about to ask his sister, who knew more about programming than he did, but she had already stepped out onto the swaying bridge. Unwilling to distract her, he whispered: "Be careful."

Liz walked slowly across the bridge, testing every step before she put her full weight on it. The detail was amazing. The bridge was constructed of thick hemp rope, the main strands as big as her wrist. Tiny curling hairs came off the rope as she gripped it. Rough-cut, uneven planks had been woven into the ropes to form the bridge. She could see the grain in the wood, dark knots, even splinters rising up from the timber. This type of detail was as good as anything she or BJ could do. Only a master programmer could have designed this bridge.

Liz pressed her foot onto a plank of wood, which immediately snapped beneath her weight and went spinning down into the chasm below. Tiny black insects scuttled away from the broken wood. The girl smiled. That was a nice touch.

"Liz . . . Liz, are you all right?"

"I'm fine. Be careful when you're coming across," she added. "Some of these planks are rotten."

The girl stopped halfway across, feeling the bridge sway beneath her. There was a thick, sulphurous rotten-egg odor coming up from below, and she could feel a warm breeze wash across her skin. She took another step forward and felt the bridge lurch, throwing her to one side. Holding tightly on to the rope, she willed herself to stand still and wait for the bridge to stop shivering.

"Move!" BJ suddenly screamed. "It's breaking up!"

Liz half-turned—just as two of the thick cords snapped, tilting the whole bridge to one side. She wrapped her hands round the thick ropes and held on desperately. In a normal VR game the player couldn't die—but this wasn't a normal VR game. She knew if she died in this game, she might slip into a VR coma in the real world, a coma from which she might never awaken. And if she fell, plummeting down into the darkness, where would it end? Was there an end?

Another rope snapped, the thick cord whipping past her face. The whole bridge tilted sideways, leaving her dangling out over the pit, the ropes burning into her flesh as she attempted to hang on. "BJ!" she screamed.

BJ's fingers were dancing across the colored buttons, creating line after line of computer code, feeding it directly into Harper's mainframe computer. "Hang on," he whispered desperately, though he knew Liz wouldn't be able to hear him.

The world began to change.

The gaping chasm disappeared as if it had been rubbed out, solid earth filling the gap. The ground—a square of soft green grass—rushed up beneath the dangling girl, catching her, just as the last strands snapped!

Liz opened her eyes, then patted the soft earth beneath her in disbelief. BJ raced over and knelt by her side. "Are you OK?"

Liz nodded shakily. She wrapped her arms around her body, trying to control the trembling in her hands, and looked around. "You reprogrammed."

"I deleted the chasm. I didn't have a choice," he added with a shaky grin. His fingers moved again and the metal sleeve blipped. "I've locked down this portion of the game. It cannot be altered now. I've also tagged it so that any virus that attaches itself to the control sequence will become infected with a virus of my own." He grinned, showing strong white teeth. "It will virus the virus."

"This game isn't virused," Liz said softly. "It's completely corrupted. We're up against something very different here."

Her brother nodded. Tilting his arm, he allowed her to read the pulsing lights on the metal sleeve. "According to this, the chasm and the lightning strike earlier were all part of the game."

"So what do we do now?" Liz asked.

"We can exit."

The girl shook her head. "If we exit now, it will give the virus a chance to spread and prepare new surprises for us. We should push on toward the *Night's Castle*." She looked around and shivered. She was intimately familiar with the landscape of *Night's Castle*. She had spent a year designing it, modeling it on maps and charts of a place called Transylvania, which had once been part of the European nation of Hungary. Now, everything looked vaguely threatening. When she and BJ had designed the world, had they made those mountains so dark and forbidding? Were the trees so tall, the bushes so twisted and warped, and the ground so rough? Where did their world end and the virused creation begin?

"I'm cold," she said, rubbing her hands together.

Although she knew that her body was lying on a metal bed in Harper's room, her brain accepted the fact that she was standing in the middle of a chill and barren landscape. And the breeze from the mountains was bitterly cold, flecked with ice and the promise of more rain. "We didn't make it so cold, did we?"

BJ shook his head. They had created the game to be challenging, not impossible and uncomfortable to play. His teeth started to chatter. His fingers moved stiffly over the glowing buttons. Clothes flowed down Liz's body—a thick fur-lined jacket with a deep hood, gloves, heavy woolen trousers, high fur-lined boots. He duplicated the string of commands and soon he was wearing the same clothes. His brain, accepting the fact that he had warm clothing, increased his body temperature.

BJ looked around. "Where *is* Ariel?"

Liz shrugged. "I haven't seen her."

"Where's Ariel?" BJ shouted at the sky.

No answer.

"Time?" he called.

12:15:02 blinked redly in the sky.

"I know we've only spent fifteen minutes in this world but already I'm beginning to hate it," he muttered.

"We made it," Liz reminded him.

BJ shook his head firmly. "We didn't make *this* world!"

"Who did then?" his sister demanded. "Only an incredibly powerful programmer could have created these effects."

✳   ✳   ✳

Ariel stood on the tallest tower in the *Night's Castle*. The castle was situated at the top of a hill, surrounded on all sides by a dark, sinister-looking forest. She was aware of the entire *Night's Castle* VR world around her. If she closed her eyes, she could actually see the thousands of lines of computer code that created this world as glowing pulses of light, flickering, darting, dancing. *Night's Castle* was a very complex game, and yet Ariel could visualize it in its entirety. She was so familiar with it now that she could even tell the difference between the portion of the game Liz had created and BJ's pieces.

Opening her eyes, returning to the computer-generated image of the castle in the forest, she was aware that the twins were somewhere below. She knew they had managed to cross the chasm—she had actually *felt* BJ change the structure of the world when he had deleted the abyss.

Concentrating hard, she stared at the forest, and it gradually faded to nothing more than a sketchy line drawing. She spotted BJ and Liz immediately. They had just reached the first marker that pointed to the High and the Low roads. The High Road was the quicker to the castle, but it was dangerous; the Low Road was longer and safer, though it had its fair share of dangers.

Ariel allowed the colors and shapes to flow back into the forest while she waited for them to make a decision.

17

"HIGH ROAD OR LOW ROAD?" BJ asked.

"Oh, you take the High Road . . . and I'll take the Low Road . . ." Liz sang, with a grin.

They stood at the very edge of the wood. On the chart that accompanied the game it was called the Twilight Wood. The marker was nothing more than a flat plank nailed at an angle onto one of the trees. HIGH ROAD had been carved roughly into the left-hand arm of the plank; the words LOW ROAD could just be made out against the weathered wood. But the track it pointed to was broader, less threatening.

"If we take the Low Road," BJ said carefully, "we have nothing to worry about until we encounter the goblins guarding the bridge. Once we get past them, we can free Pegasus, the flying horse, and fly straight to the castle. If we don't free Pegasus, it will mean making our way through the Marsh of Sighs, and that means we'll have to answer the boatman's riddle."

"How many riddles did you program into the boatman?" Liz asked.

"Two thousand," BJ said quickly. "And they're

randomly generated, so there's no way of predicting what you're going to be asked."

Liz stepped forward and squinted up the length of the High Road. It disappeared into shadow almost as soon as it entered the forest. "Remind me what little surprises we put on the High Road," she said.

"Everything," BJ replied with a grimace. "First the werewolves, then the Golem, the Mud Monster, the vampire bats, the fire-breathing dragon, the . . ."

Liz held up her hand, silencing him. "What was the first one again?"

"The werewolves . . ." BJ said.

Even as he was speaking, a dozen enormous gray furred and red-eyed wolves appeared out of the shadows of the trees.

". . . but they don't appear unless you're playing this game at night," he finished, lamely.

The pack leader, a huge gray-haired wolf, threw back its head and howled. The cry was taken up by the rest of the pack, and then, from deep in the heart of the forest, the cries were returned by a second wolf pack. A third pack took up the howling until it sounded as if the entire forest was full of the savage gray wolves.

"There should be only one wolf pack," BJ muttered.

"Forget what there should be!" Liz pushed her hood back off her head. "Delete them," she snapped. "Do it now!"

The wolf pack was advancing on the twins. Some walked on four paws, but others, those who were half-man half-wolf, walked on their hind legs.

BJ's fingers danced across the glimmering studs on his

arm. One by one, the werewolves winked out of existence.

And immediately reappeared!

There was movement in the trees behind the wolves, and the forest came alive with whispering rustles. Red eyes glowed in the shadows, vanishing when BJ erased the computer text, reappearing a heartbeat later.

"Stop!" Liz said urgently. "No more. Every time you delete one, two come back."

The wolf pack was now enormous: fifty huge wolves and at least twenty of the man-wolves. One, bigger than the rest, moved through the pack. Although he walked on his hind legs, his features were still those of a savage wolf. His teeth were long and sharp but his hands were human, long-fingered, long-nailed. Reaching behind his back, he procured a saw-toothed dagger and then slowly licked his lips. Raising the dagger high, with cold gray light running down the length of the blade, the pack leader pointed straight at the twins. Although no words were spoken, the pack surged forward, howling savagely.

BJ's fingers moved on the metal sleeve—and the ground opened up in front of the wolves.

The pack fell yelping and yapping into the deep pit. Most of the wolves vanished before they reached the bottom, but the werewolves began to climb up the high crumbling sides of the pit, snapping and snarling. The six wolves and two werewolves who hadn't fallen into the hole immediately darted off left and right, obviously seeking a way around the pit.

"We'll take the Low Road," Liz said quickly, backing away from the edge of the pit.

BJ didn't answer. His fingers were stabbing across the controls, and there was a slight sheen of sweat on his forehead.

"What's wrong?" Liz began, and then stopped. She could see what was happening. The pit was vanishing, the edges growing fuzzy and indistinct, the rough ground reappearing. BJ regained control of the game for a few seconds and the pit opened up again, but the opposite edge immediately began to close in.

"I can't control it," he whispered, fear making his voice crack. He had first played and then created VR worlds since he was a young boy. They had always been safe because he had always been in control.

Liz caught his arm and pulled him away from the edge of the pit. When they turned around, four huge were-wolves reared up in front of them, teeth and ragged claws slashing, razor-sharp knives flickering . . .

The world stopped.

BJ and Liz awoke in Harper's control room. The small man's round face swam into view. "I thought it was time to take you out of there," he said gently.

❋   ❋   ❋

Ariel watched the werewolves advance upon the twins. She shuddered as BJ opened up the pit. He had created the effect in desperation and his codes were crude and ugly, unlike his usually smooth and mathematically correct inputs. Because it had been created so quickly, Ariel guessed that the pit would be unstable and wouldn't be able to resist the virus. She saw it disappear as the virus regained control of the VR world, and then the twins turned and the werewolves loomed up before them. The girl was wondering whether she should act when the twins vanished.

Pounding her fists into the hard castle battlements, she said aloud, "Time?"

12:28:22 blinked in the sky. The twins had lasted less than half an hour in the world they had created.

Nodding in satisfaction, Ariel removed herself from the game. It was just as she had suspected: the twins' reputation had been blown out of all proportion by the media. They had lasted twenty-eight minutes, whereas she had previously survived for more than two hours in the deadly game.

✳   ✳   ✳

Miles away, one of the lights on the glowing map of the city winked out.

"Computer usage has now ceased," the artificial voice reported.

Captain Lyons gritted his teeth in frustration. He forced himself to remain calm, knowing that the computers monitored all officers' stress levels. He didn't want to be pulled off the case just now for some enforced sick time. "Have you located the source?" he asked.

"The computer usage is routed through several machines. Power is drawn from numerous sources and concealed by using a series of switchbacks and false addresses. However, the search area has been reduced to one-thousand-square-yard block of the Quays. The search will continue when the computer usage resumes."

Lyons turned away from the screen, keeping his face flat and expressionless. He was close, so close. But while one thousand square yards didn't seem a large area, the

Quays were such a warren of streets, alleys, lanes, cellars, and basements that they could hold from one thousand to three thousand people. The twins could be anywhere.

Maybe his mysterious caller, the same person who had warned him that the twins were entering the VR world, would contact him again. Someone on the Quays was sheltering the twins. He was convinced of it. But someone else was prepared to betray them.

The three o'clock news carried a fifteen-second story.

"Police now believe that the O'Connor twins, owners of Gemini Corporation, who were accused of creating an illegal and potentially lethal game, have gone into hiding on the Quays. A reward of half a million credits has been offered for information leading to their capture."

18

SITTING AT THE ROUND METAL TABLE across from Harper and Ariel, the twins spooned up plates of gray food substitute. They were both so hungry they didn't notice the look or texture of the food.

BJ scraped his plate clean and wiped his mouth with a paper tissue. "VR always gives me a great appetite," he said.

"That's because your brain thinks it's doing all those things you did in the VR world," Aaron Harper said. "Even though your body is doing nothing, your brain thinks it's burning up calories and therefore you should be hungry."

"Have you any idea what happened in there?" Liz asked Harper, although her eyes were on the girl.

"I think the game is completely corrupted." He shrugged. "The code is running wild. You saw that yourself when you attempted to delete the werewolves: they simply multiplied. The virus intercepted your minus symbol and made it into a plus."

"So what do we do?" Liz wondered.

"It's far too dangerous to return to the game . . ." Harper said slowly. He nodded at the metal sleeve resting on the beside BJ. "You can't even reprogram from within the game."

"What about you, Ariel?" Liz said.

The black-eyed girl stared sullenly at the twins. Colors shimmered across her eyes like oil on water.

"Where were you?"

"I've played the game before. I was able to enter it at my last saved position, on the battlements of *Night's Castle*," Ariel whispered. "I simply waited for you there."

"You could have told us," snapped BJ.

"You didn't experience anything unusual then?" Liz asked.

The girl shook her head.

BJ looked up. "But you're connected directly into the computer. Didn't you sense that something was wrong?"

Ariel shook her head again. "The machine thinks everything is as it should be. The virus is camouflaged within the normal game code; it's impossible to spot. I think," she added, glancing sidelong at her father, "that this is one of the new intelligent viruses."

There was a moment of shocked silence. Then Harper said: "You have heard of the intelligent viruses?"

The twins nodded, an identical movement of their heads.

Harper steepled his fingers in front of his face. "Let me recap. As you know, there have always been viruses in the computer world. The earliest ones probably began as a practical joke, but soon we all realized that they had a serious side to them. We learned how to deal with viruses that swallow up computer memory or destroy programs or jumble information, even those that wreck a machine's memory. Some of us have come across viruses that can change their configuration on a daily basis, so the virus you're looking for today has a completely different identity tomorrow."

"But we know how to trap most of those viruses and wipe them off the machines," BJ said.

"Practically all of them," Harper agreed, "even those that change themselves. But an intelligent virus is a little different. An intelligent virus has the ability to 'learn.'" He smiled sadly. "Your parents once experimented with intelligent viruses, thinking they could be put to some good use."

"And could they?" Liz wondered.

Harper shook his head. "The accident that killed your parents stopped that experiment." He took a deep breath. "When you deleted the chasm from the game today, BJ, the virus *learned* that you could remove certain portions of the game code. I'm only guessing now," he added, "but I imagine that it immediately protected the rest of the code so that pieces could not be removed."

"So when I deleted the werewolves, it simply brought them back," the boy said.

Harper nodded. "And then turned the command around and created a dozen more. Then you created a pit between you and the creatures. However, earlier you had removed a pit. So it reversed what you had done, and removed your pit."

"What would have happened if you hadn't pulled us out then?" Liz asked.

Harper's expression turned grim. "It's hard to say. If the werewolves had *killed* you—in other words, if your

103

brains had assumed that you had died—you would have fallen into a VR coma." Lacing his fingers together, he sat back into his chair.

"So what do we do now?" BJ wondered.

Harper shrugged.

Ariel leaned forward across the table. "You can't go back into *Night's Castle*. You wouldn't survive."

Liz closed her eyes and ran her hands across her close-cropped hair. "Are all the copies of *Night's Castle* virused in this way?" she wondered aloud.

"They couldn't be," BJ said. "Otherwise we would have a lot more people in VR comas."

"To prove our innocence to Department 13, we need to show that someone has deliberately virused certain copies of the game . . ." Liz continued.

"And the only way to do that is to isolate the virus," BJ added.

"And once we do that, we can neutralize it and release those people who are now in a coma," Liz finished, opening her eyes.

"Previously, only those players who had made it to the castle were afflicted," Harper said, "but obviously the virus has now spread to all aspects of the game."

Liz sighed. "We'll have to go back into the game," she said quietly.

BJ touched the metal sleeve on the table. "But I can't take this with us. Every time I use it, the machine will either duplicate or reverse what I'm attempting to do. We'll be defenseless."

"Not quite," Harper said quickly. "In the same way that you created warm clothes for yourselves in there, I can

104

create weapons and armor for you. And I'll try to place you as close to the castle as possible."

"We'll rest first," Liz announced, knowing her brother would want to go immediately.

"You realize that once you're in the VR world," Harper reminded them, "there's a very good chance you won't be able to leave—unless you defeat the virus."

"We know that," Liz said softly. "We don't have a choice. If we don't prove our innocence, we will either spend the rest of our lives on the run or locked in a VR prison."

19

"YOU DON'T HAVE TO GO BACK IN with them," Harper said, watching Ariel closely. The girl was standing in front of the banks of computer screens looking at the twins.

She turned slowly, her eyes reflecting red light from the monitors. "I have to go," she murmured. "Someone has to take care of them."

✳   ✳   ✳

"There's no need for both of us to go," Liz said, lying on the hard metal cot with her hands behind her head, staring at the low rusting ceiling.

BJ mumbled groggily. He wasn't long awake, and his dreams had been disturbed by terrifying nightmares in which he had been chased by shadowy creatures. Every time he had managed to escape his pursuers, the ground had opened up beneath his feet and he had fallen . . . fallen . . . fallen.

"Are you listening to me?" Liz asked.

"Yes. Yes," BJ said quickly, sitting up, yawning, and stretching his arms wide. "I'm listening to you." He glanced at the tiny watch on his right wrist. He was surprised to find that he had slept for eight hours, but he was still tired.

"I said there's no need for both of us to go back into the VR world. One of us should stay here in case anything happens."

BJ swung his legs out of bed and turned to look at his sister. "What do you mean: in case anything happens?"

"You know what I mean," she said calmly.

"You mean if one of us gets killed in the game," BJ snapped. "And what happens then?"

Surprised by the anger in his voice, Liz sat up and looked at her brother.

"What am I going to do if you go into the game and get killed there?" BJ demanded. "What am I going to do?"

Liz reached out and took her brother's hand, squeezing the fingers gently. The twins had always been close, and since their parents' death they had become even closer. It was this same closeness, the ability to think and act alike, that made them such successful Game Makers.

"If anything happens to you," BJ said, looking into his sister's bright gray eyes, "I'll have no one left."

Liz nodded. "Those were my thoughts too," she said with a grim smile. "I didn't want you to go into the game because I was afraid that something might happen to you . . ."

"And I was afraid that if you went into the game something would happen to you. So, it's decided," he said firmly, "neither of us will go, or . . ."

"We'll both go," Liz said decisively.

"And we'll both come back!"

*   *   *

Captain Lyons came awake with a start as the phone beside his bed began chiming insistently. He hit the switch with the heel of his hand, bringing the screen alive. The police logo was replaced by flickering bands of distorted colors, which finally settled into a blank gray-black screen. A series of numbers scrolled across the top of the screen: the call had been received five minutes ago, coming from a public box on the edge of the Quays. It had come into the station as a personal call, but he had requested that all calls be transferred to his apartment. The central computer had routinely stored the message and then switched it through.

The screen remained blank, and Lyons realized that the camera facility, which should have shown him his caller, had been disabled and the voice distorted electronically. The message was as brief as the previous one: *"The O'Connor twins will enter the VR world of* Night's Castle *within the hour."*

Lyons threw back the single sheet and hurried into the tiny bathroom. There was a triumphant grin on his narrow face: he knew they were on the Quays, he knew which sector. Once they began using their computer, it would be a matter of moments before his department traced it to its source.

20

"THIS TIME, WHEN YOU ENTER the VR world, there's no turning back," Aaron Harper said as the twins lay down on the narrow metal tables. The screens banked behind him were alive with flowing lines of numbers and jagged, multicolored patterns, while a single screen slowly counted down from sixty to zero.

"I have adapted some of the game's code," he added, "which should allow me to provide you with weapons and armor. I'm not sure how long they'll last, but you will have to realize that sooner or later the virus in the game will interfere in some way with them, leaving you defenseless."

He turned his attention to Ariel, who stood ready to reenter the VR world. "Be careful," he warned. "Use your special power wisely. I want you all back safely."

BJ had pulled on his flesh-soft gloves but paused before putting on the goggles. "Try to place us as close to the castle as possible."

Harper nodded. "I've devised a way of bypassing the opening sequences." He glanced over his shoulder at the screen, which showed the countdown.

Twenty . . . nineteen . . . eighteen . . .

"Do you know what you're looking for?" Harper asked.

"Not really." BJ grinned. "All we know is that it will be right in the very core of the castle, because that's the most complex part of the game."

"Five seconds," announced Ariel suddenly, reaching in under her hair to plug in the snaking red cord. She breathed deeply, her eyelids squeezing tightly shut as she entered the VR world.

BJ and Liz settled the narrow VR goggles onto their faces, abruptly seeing a gray emptiness that was shot through with jagged lines of white and yellow static. In their ears, a high-pitched voice set their teeth on edge.

Harper's voice echoed in the distance. "You will experience some interference because I'm beginning the game at a later stage. Rather than rewrite the game code and possibly activate the virus, I simply speeded it up, so the first forty minutes has been condensed into twenty-eight seconds. You may feel some nausea, so perhaps it would be better if you closed your eyes . . .

"Good luck," he added. He finished the countdown. "Three, two, one . . ."

His voice faded off into a ghostly crackle.

In the twins' goggles the lines of static grew even more frenzied. Irregular spots and splashes of brilliant color burst against their eyelids. The colors were so bright they were almost painful.

Then they were falling . . . falling . . . falling, air screaming past their faces, sucking their breath away, drowning out their own cries. The sense of downward movement stopped a heartbeat before the sudden, abrupt silence. A second later, sensations returned and they became aware of the sound of gentle gurgling.

Moisture spattered across their faces, making them blink in surprise. They were lying side-by-side on damp grass beside a fast-flowing river. Drops of water washing against the river bank splashed onto them. The illusion was so perfect that they could actually feel the icy water trickling down their necks, the droplets cold and wet against their faces, moist against their lips.

BJ rolled over, sitting up with a groan. He looked around for Ariel but couldn't see her. He hoped she hadn't ended up in the river. Coming slowly, stiffly to his feet, he turned to help his sister stand . . . and stopped, blinking furiously. Liz's outline was indistinct and shimmering, almost as if he were looking at her through a heat haze. He touched his face, rubbing the heel of his hand into his eyes, wondering if the VR goggles were faulty, though the rest of the world was crystal-clear.

"BJ?" Liz whispered. She was frozen to the ground, unable to move a muscle, even blink her eyes. "What's happening to me, BJ?" She struggled unsuccessfully to keep the note of fear from her voice. Had she been infected by the virus already? Was this how it was to slip into a VR coma?

As BJ watched, tiny white and gray lines darted across his sister's arms and legs, flicking around her fingers, gathering on her chest, shoulders, and thighs in pools of silver light, slowly hardening into a cold metallic skin. Long-fingered metal gloves covered her hands; knee-high silver boots with toes that came to sharp spikes appeared on her feet. A long saw-toothed sword materialized on the ground beside her, and a razor-edged throwing boomerang popped out of the thin air directly in front of BJ and dropped onto the ground.

BJ suddenly realized what was happening. "It's all right. Harper's duplicating the weapons and armor of one of the warriors in the castle."

The armor and weapons solidified, and Liz suddenly found she could move. BJ hauled her to her feet with an effort, the metallic armor clinking softly. He tapped it, shaking his head in admiration. "It's a brilliant construction."

"I designed the armor," Liz reminded him.

"So you did."

The girl was clad from the neck downward in what looked like a smooth and seamless metal skin that mirrored the surroundings. BJ could see his own distorted reflection on its surface. Although her head was bare, a high collar rose up to protect the back of her skull.

BJ bent and picked up the sword, testing the edge by slashing at some of the high grass that bordered the river. Strands of cut grass whirled away into the water.

"How does it feel?" he asked, handing her the sword, hilt first.

"Comfortable," she nodded. She suddenly looked doubtful. "But will it work?"

"It has exactly the same existence in this world as everything else, so why shouldn't it?" he said, lifting the boomerang. "Did you design this?"

Liz nodded. "This is the bonus weapon from level two." She slid the long sword into a scabbard over her left shoulder and stretched out a gloved hand for the boomerang. "It was a weapon used by the indigenous Australian people. I simply adapted it slightly." Catching the boomerang at one end, she cocked her arm back and threw. The metal wing hissed as it flew through the air, slicing cleanly through a dozen finger-thick branches before it curved around and came back to Liz. It clanged into her hand with the sound of metal against metal.

"I wonder how long it will be before the virus renders all this useless?"

BJ shrugged. "Well, we know that, technically, the virus can affect anything and everything within the VR world. However, it is more likely to be attracted to unusual or new pieces of programming. What Harper has done is to take some of the existing program and use it elsewhere. It's clever." He nodded quickly. "It should work."

"But what about you?" Liz asked. "Isn't he going to give you any armor or weapons?"

BJ looked down. He was still wearing the one-piece suit he'd worn in the real world. "Obviously not," he shrugged—and stopped. Something had just trickled down his back, like icy water. He worked his shoulders, reaching around awkwardly to scratch between his shoulder blades—and snatched his hands away as pins and needles shot through his fingers.

He looked up at his sister. She was staring intently at him. "Turn around," she said quietly.

BJ turned and looked at the fast-flowing water. The icy tickling on his back became almost unbearable. He felt as if a tight band had closed around his chest, and a heavy weight settled across his shoulders, making him hunch forward. Tiny white sparks danced across his chest in a big X shape. "Liz, what is it?" he asked, wondering why he was whispering. The white sparks buzzing on his chest disappeared abruptly.

"It's over," Liz said.

BJ looked down: two leather straps crisscrossed his chest over his shoulders and hooked onto a broad leather belt. He reached around behind his back and touched something hard and cold. Metal. He traced hard iron and smoothly polished wood, but it was only when he touched a trigger that he recognized the shape. "It's a crossbow!"

His sister's armor creaked slightly as she moved up behind him. She unhooked the weapon from its shoulder harness as he turned, and handed it to him.

"I don't remember creating this," he said, turning the heavy crossbow around in his hands.

"Yes, you did," Liz said quickly. "Remember when we decided that the guards on the *Night's Castle* needed a weapon that was effective over a long distance?"

BJ nodded. The crossbows had been a very late addition to the game, when the twins discovered that there was no point in putting guards on the castle walls if players could walk unchallenged right up to the gate.

"Your clothes are different," Liz said.

BJ looked down. He had been concentrating on the changes taking place on his back, so he hadn't noticed

114

that Harper had altered his clothes, dressing him in the outfit of one of the forest brigands: leather trousers, leather tunic, and high leather boots. There was a long-bladed knife in a sheath on his hip. He ran the flat of his hand down the leather: it felt smooth as silk.

"If we get out of this alive," he said, "we should write a little program that allows players to choose from a wardrobe of clothes."

"That's a great idea. But first, let's concentrate on getting out of here." She looked around. "Do you have any idea where we are?"

BJ cradled the crossbow in his arms. "The only river in this world is the Styx. It flows through the Twilight Wood and into the Marsh of Sighs." He crouched by the river's edge and looked at the fast-flowing water, pointing down to the left. "It's traveling in that direction, which means *Night's Castle* lies in this direction."

Liz followed her brother's pointing finger. "How far are we from the castle?"

BJ shrugged. "Not far. We'll follow the river upstream. Once we're out of the trees, we should be able to see the castle on the hill."

Liz shaded her eyes with her hand. "There's something on the water . . ." she said.

BJ squinted into the distance. "I can't see anything except the cloud." He stopped suddenly, realizing that he wasn't looking at a cloud but at something that was churning the water to a white froth.

Liz caught her brother's arm, pulling him away from the river bank. "What did you put in the river?" she asked desperately.

"Nothing. A few fish, small electric eels," he said, glancing over his shoulder. The churning white water was drawing closer. Metal sparkled in the midst of the foam, and BJ stopped, squinting to make out the shape. There was something familiar about it . . .

"BJ! Come on!"

BJ was turning as the creature rose up out of the water.

21

THE CREATURE HAD ONCE BEEN AN EEL or a worm, but the virus had twisted and altered its shape and size, turning it into something far more deadly. It was at least sixteen feet long, with a flattened blunt head that opened into a perfectly circular mouth filled with rows of triangular teeth. There were no eyes, but a series of delicate waving fronds ringed the mouth. The fronds fixed on the twins' position, shivering in the still air—then the creature heaved up out of the water, rippling toward them.

"This wasn't in our game," Liz whispered. "What is it?"

BJ shook his head. "I don't know. But remember, this isn't really our game anymore." Beads of sweat popped out on his bald skull as he struggled to pull back the long handle that cocked the crossbow. The cord finally slid into place with a click, and he fumbled with the short, stubby crossbow bolts, dropping one into the slot.

"It's got armor plating on its skin," Liz said in wonder.

BJ spun around, lifted the heavy crossbow, and sighted on the creature. His sister was right: there was a scattering of irregular metallic plates on the creature's leathery gray-white skin. "It looks a bit like your armor," he said.

"When Harper was dressing us, he must have activated the virus . . ." Liz began.

"And it mutated this creature and added the armor," BJ finished. He pulled the curved trigger and the crossbow twanged. The short, thick bolt hurtled through the air and clanged off an irregular circle of armor beneath the creature's throat. The eel stiffened, it fronds standing straight out, its mouth opening wide, revealing a long throat, ridged with muscle. When its mouth closed, BJ and Liz clearly heard its teeth rasp together. The creature curled in on itself, then rose up almost to its full height, towering over the twins.

"Run!" BJ shouted, pushing Liz aside.

The creature flopped down again, crashing onto the ground where, only seconds before, they'd both been standing.

Liz dragged her boomerang free, turned, and flung it at the creature in one smooth move. It sliced neatly through a chunk of flesh high on the creature's back, continued on into a high arc, and returned to Liz's outstretched hand. It was covered in a thick, gooey jelly. The creature's mouth opened wide in a soundless scream, and a violent shuddering rippled through its entire body, its thrashing tail scattering trees and bushes. In quick succession, two crossbow bolts thudded into its side. The eel jerked away from the sting, crashing into a tall elm tree, uprooting it in a shower of earth and stones.

Liz saw the tree falling and turned to run. Leaves and branches rained down upon her—and then two thick branches struck her across the small of the back, driving her forward onto the ground. A long, sharp branch speared into the earth inches from her face. Liz struggled to come to her feet, wincing with the pain across her back. Her armor had protected her from serious injury, but she guessed she would be black and blue with bruises and briefly wondered if her physical body back in the real world would also carry the bruises. She tasted copper in her mouth and realized she had bitten into the inside of her cheek. She could move the upper half of her body, but there was a weight pressing down on her legs. Twisting around awkwardly, she saw that they were trapped beneath the tree trunk. A couple of thick branches had prevented the trunk from crushing them into the ground.

The eel moved closer, its huge head turning from side to side. Its fronds waved as it tasted the air, sorting through the dozens of odors, analyzing them until it detected the rich smell of blood. It undulated forward, head dipping into the fallen tree, tendrils dancing across the leaves and branches, identifying them. A frond slid across Liz's face from cheek to ear, leaving a slimy trail on her skin. The touch drove the creature into a frenzy. It attacked the barrier of branches, teeth snapping, in an effort to get to the trapped girl. Liz attempted to drag her sword free, but it was trapped at an awkward angle. The eel was almost on top of her now, its teeth—and they were metal, she realized, triangular slivers of metal— snapping wood, the air around her filled with sap and resin. In another moment, its metal teeth were going to close around her leg . . .

Liz opened her mouth and screamed.

BJ fired his last bolt into the creature's ridged back, but it didn't even flinch. Flinging the crossbow aside, he dragged his knife free and raced toward the eel.

"Harper," he shouted, "help us!"

* * *

Sitting before the bank of glowing monitors, Aaron Harper desperately stabbed at the switch that terminated the game.

Nothing happened.

He pressed it again, then tried another sequence of commands to close down the machine and end the game. None of the commands worked; the switches didn't respond: the virus had control of the program.

He could only watch in horror as the eel snapped through the last barrier separating it from the girl. He heard the boy's cry for help, saw him launch himself onto the creature's back, stabbing at it with his knife. The eel's muscles rippled, and the boy went flying backward, crashing onto the ground, where he lay still and unmoving.

Harper leaned forward and pressed a switch that blanked the monitors: there was nothing he could do, and he didn't want to see what was going to happen next.

* * *

The eel's metallic teeth snapped through the final branch, crushing it to ragged splinters. Its fronds moved across Liz's face, rasping on her close-cropped hair, brushing stickily against the metal armor. It hesitated, as if trying to distinguish the difference between soft flesh and hard metal. A frond waved in front of the girl's eyes. Liz suddenly caught it in a gloved hand and tugged hard. The eel reared back in pain.

"So you can be hurt!" Liz's grin of triumph faded when she saw her brother lying on the ground beyond the creature.

And then the eel opened its circular mouth wide and darted toward the girl, teeth snapping toward her face.

And stopped.

It lost definition first, the tiny details blurring as if the image had gone out of focus. The colors altered, shifted, fading—brown turning to sand, red to pink, black to gray. One by one the colors vanished, the lighter colors disappearing first, leaving square "holes" in the creature. In a matter of heartbeats, the terrifying eel had been reduced to a series of white lines, squares, and rectangles.

And then these too vanished.

For a single moment the entire fabric of the virtual reality world shivered, the colors lost their subtle shading, shadows vanished, and everything took on a flat two-dimensional quality. Liz caught a glimpse of long, scrolling lines of computer code shivering across the sky, and then the world settled itself, like a badly tuned viewer coming back into focus.

Ariel stepped up to Liz and crouched down in front of her. The girl's solid black eyes gave her a sinister expression when she smiled.

"Lucky for you I showed up," she said hoarsely.

22

THE HEAVILY ARMORED POLICE CRUISER moved slowly through the narrow Quay streets. Police vehicles were a rare sight here and always meant trouble. The thickly packed streets emptied rapidly as the people vanished into the narrow alleyways and lanes where the cruiser couldn't follow. Shops closed down, the owners hanging heavy wooden shutters across the thick plastic, while metal grilles slid into place over the fronts of the luxury shops.

Within ten minutes, the Quays were still and deserted. The noise of the cruiser's motor echoed off the walls, sounding like an animal's growl.

Inside, Captain Lyons sat hunched over the glowing monitor, its green light giving his face a diseased appearance. With tiny, precise movements, he traced the location of the computer power usage, rapidly narrowing it down street by street, alley by alley.

"Take the next right," he ordered.

He had a hundred troops waiting just outside the Quays. Once he had the twins' location, he would flood the area with officers. This time, they would not escape.

"Left!"

The blip on his computer screen solidified into a firm white light. He had them! Captain Eddie Lyons smiled triumphantly. He spoke into the tiny microphone in the collar of his uniform. "Officers to my location!"

As he climbed out of the cruiser, he could hear the helicopter troop-carriers coming closer. Looking up, he spotted the opening high in the wall. That was where he would find the twins!

23

"HOW DID YOU DO THAT?" Liz asked shakily, scrubbing at her face, where she could still feel the creature's slimy touch on her skin. She felt a wave of relief wash over her as she saw BJ come shakily to his feet.

Ariel's smile was cold as she hauled Liz up. "Don't forget I am part of this world, part of the machine. I am the machine. I simply destroyed the lines of game code that controlled the eel."

"But when we did that," BJ said, limping over, "the machine simply recreated the lines."

Ariel's black eyes looked like holes in her head. "I didn't delete them," she said softly. "I destroyed them. Surely you know that when information is deleted from a computer memory, it can be undeleted with the proper program. That's how the machine recreated the items you erased. When I deleted the code, I then overwrote it, destroying it completely, ensuring that it could not recreate the eel."

"But how?" Liz demanded. "How do you communicate with the machine?"

"I thought about it! In this world, I can make my thoughts

real." She spread her arms wide and turned her face to the sky. "In this world, I am a goddess," she said savagely.

Liz glanced quickly at her brother. He caught her alarmed look and nodded slightly. He, too, was coming to the conclusion that Ariel wasn't entirely sane.

＊　　＊　　＊

The *Night's Castle*, grim and forbidding, appeared as soon as they cleared the forest, crowning the top of a barren mountain and dominating the entire countryside. Dozens of pointed spires and turrets rose into the sky, which had been designed to remain permanently black with thunderclouds.

"It looks a bit scary," Liz said softly.

"Exactly," BJ agreed with a proud grin. He turned to look at Ariel. "What do you think?" he asked.

The pale-faced girl raised her head to look at the castle. "I see lines of computer code," she said coldly and walked away.

Liz shaded her eyes and looked at the castle again. When they were making the game, they had created the most frightening fortress they could imagine: dripping black stone walls streaked with moss, rusted iron gates, crumbling towers, an empty, overgrown moat. "There's something different about it," she said very softly, almost to herself, "something strange."

BJ caught her hand, pulling her away. "It's not the castle that's changed," he said, "it's the game. Now that you know the game is virused, you're looking at the castle in a new light."

Liz shivered, her metal armor creaking. "Do we have to go inside?"

125

"The people who fell into the VR coma all reached the castle. Whatever 'killed' them is in there. We have to face it and defeat it—and hope we recognize the strain of virus," he added.

"And stay alive," Liz reminded him.

"I hadn't forgotten," he said with a grin. He turned and pointed ahead toward Ariel. "Come on. Let's try to stick together."

The path they were following was little more than a broken track up the mountainside. They were forced to pick their way slowly and carefully across the rock-strewn surface, choosing every step with care: a slip could twist or snap an ankle. Ariel moved smoothly across the track, her eyes fixed firmly on the castle.

BJ pointed to a twisted tree beside the path. "As we pass that marker, the thunder and lightning begins," he reminded Liz.

Ariel was in the lead, but there was no reaction when she passed the marker.

BJ stopped before the tree. Liz crouched down beside him, her hand on his back. "There's something about her . . ." he muttered.

Liz nodded. "Something very strange." She straightened up. "But let's see what happens," she said, as she stepped past the tree.

A low rumble of thunder boomed across the sky. Lightning flashed behind the castle, highlighting it in silver and black.

"Well, at least that still works," BJ said, following his sister down the track. He had programmed in five peals of thunder and double that number of lightning strikes. The

126

last three were forked lightning that would come to earth behind the castle.

"Three . . . four . . . five," he counted the rumbling crashes of thunder. "That's it," he began, and then stopped. Another peal of thunder had rumbled across the sky. Lightning flashed again, closer now, the air suddenly rich with the stench of ozone. There was a tremendous crackle of electricity almost directly overhead, and a jagged spear of light drove into the ground to their right, showering them with stones and pebbles. BJ heard the grit rattle off Liz's armor.

That was wrong!

BJ stopped, shocked by a sudden terrifying thought: his sister was wearing metal armor! He was running even before the thunder crashed across the sky, his cry of warning lost in the incredible noise. He hit Liz in the small of the back, the force of the blow and her metal armor numbing his entire arm from the shoulder downward. He sent her sprawling forward and rolled away, just as a second jagged spear of light hit the ground where she had been standing, churning the earth to a smoking mess. He attempted to rise to his feet, but his bruised arm betrayed him and he collapsed again. Thunder crashed once more, and BJ could only watch helplessly as the third jagged lightning strike hurtled toward his sister.

❋   ❋   ❋

Captain Lyons hung on the end of the swinging rope while the police helicopter maneuvered into position. When he was over the mouth of the dark opening in the Quay walls, he released the safety harness and dropped the last few feet onto the platform. Without waiting for reinforcements, he drew his pistol and advanced into the tunnel.

Aaron Harper sat before his bank of reactivated screens and monitors, his fingers moving over his keyboard in a final effort to influence the game. The next lightning strike would "kill" the girl, driving her into a VR coma. As a last desperate measure, he could disconnect her from the VR game. It was incredibly risky—the shock of coming out of the game could also drive her into a coma—but at least it gave her some chance. If the lightning hit her, she would stand no chance at all.

He was reaching for the thin red cables that connected Liz to the VR console when a cold circle of metal pressed against the back of his neck.

"Stay exactly where you are." The voice was hard and emotionless.

Harper looked up and saw Lyons reflected in the monitors. The police officer was holding a gun to the back of his head. "If I don't pull the girl out of the game, she'll go into a coma."

"Good," Lyons said callously. "She deserves to die." He pushed Harper back into the chair and then stood behind him, eagerly watching the screens.

Onscreen, lightning flashed, spearing downward.

24

TIME SLOWED . . .
   Slowed . . .
   Stopped.
   The ragged streak of lightning stopped inches from Liz's chest and then vanished, dissolving into glittering sparkles of light that buzzed and sizzled off the girl's metal armor. The ripping sound died to a metallic ping.
   Time moved on again.
   Ariel strode up, her hands on her hips. She looked down at the twins, who were cowering on the ground, and she shook her head in disgust. "I thought you two were the finest Game Makers in the world. But without me, you would both now be lying in a VR coma."
   "You saved my life," Liz said. She was about to thank the girl but Ariel interrupted.
   "I stopped the computer clock to give myself time to isolate the lines of code that controlled the final lightning strike—and then I simply destroyed the code," she stated and turned away.
   BJ helped his sister to her feet. They were both shaking

so badly that they could barely stand. "Are you OK?" he asked.

"I ache everywhere. I bet I'll have bruises when I wake up." Liz attempted a smile, which failed. She turned to look at Ariel. "That's twice she's saved my life."

Her brother nodded, his stone gray eyes narrowing as he too turned to look at the girl.

"But if she's so powerful in this world, why can't she isolate and destroy the virus?" Liz asked.

BJ nodded. "Technically, there would be nothing to stop her doing that. She's certainly powerful enough."

"It's almost as if she's playing with us," Liz whispered.

"But why?" BJ demanded. "Surely she wants to destroy this virus as much as we do?" He looked up into the sky. "Harper, I know you can hear me. Why have you and Ariel never tried to destroy the virus yourselves? Why did you allow us to come into this world when you knew we'd be helpless?"

Liz squeezed her brother's arm. "He can't answer you."

"I know that. But when I get back to the real world, I'll ask him in person." He pointed to where Ariel was striding toward the enormous castle doors. "Come on. We need to stay together. She's our only chance of surviving in this place."

*　　*　　*

Lyons turned the flat, ugly pistol toward Harper. "Tell me what happened. Why didn't the lightning hit the girl?"

The small, stout man ran his hands over his bald head, his eyes darting from screen to screen. "My daughter is also in the VR world with the twins. However, instead of wearing goggles and gloves to interface with the game, she is hooked in directly to the computer. In effect, she is part of the machine, able to do almost anything the computer is capable of." He glanced at the police officer. "You heard her: she stopped the game and removed the lightning just before it struck."

Lyons shook his head in disappointment. The tiny radio in the collar of his uniform crackled, requesting an update on his situation, but he ignored it.

Harper turned away from the screens. "Why do you hate the twins?" he asked.

Lyons's face was a carefully controlled mask. "I hate them for what they are."

"They're only Game Makers," Harper protested.

Lyons turned toward the screens, watching the twins follow Ariel through the castle's double gates, and then he swivelled around to look at the three still bodies on the narrow metal tables behind him. Something in his expression alarmed Harper, and Harper continued speaking, trying to distract him.

"Why are you picking on them? They've never made an illegal game." He jerked a thumb at the screens. "This game has been virused. They went into it in an attempt to identify and isolate the virus. Once they know what is sending people into the VR comas, they can reverse its effects. They wouldn't have done that if they were guilty . . ."

Lyons shook his head sharply. "They are guilty."

"How do you know?"

"They ran," Lyons said simply. "That shows their guilt. That shows they had something to hide."

"They needed time to investigate the game," Harper

said quickly. He stopped as Lyons's eyes widened in sudden recognition.

"I know you. You're The Harper!"

"I was once called that."

"You were a Game Maker too."

"A long time ago."

Lyons nodded very slowly. "It was people like you," he nodded at the screen, "people like them, who killed my wife."

Harper turned to look at the police officer. Lyons's expression was stone, his lips drawn into a thin line, his eyes closed to slits. The hand holding the gun began to tremble, and Harper could see the whiteness of his knuckles as his grip tightened.

"We were married less than a year," Lyons said stiffly, his eyes now fixed on the screens. The twins were moving through *Night's Castle*'s gloomy corridors, but Lyons was seeing the past. "She liked games, loved them. She could spend hours in VR. It was only later that I realized she was addicted to them." He took a deep, shuddering breath. "The doctors and psychologists have fancy names for the condition now, but on the streets they're known as burnouts. My wife was a burnout."

"What happened?" Harper asked when Lyons fell silent.

"I was abroad for a week, learning about the latest computer games," he said bitterly. "When I came home, I discovered my wife plugged into the VR console. She was dead."

"How?" Harper asked.

"The doctors told me they thought she had been

playing the game nonstop for a week. She had forgotten to eat, to drink. She'd had no sleep. Her body simply stopped functioning." He looked at the screens again, and now his eyes were wide and staring, glittering madly. "She was playing *Magician's Law*, a Gemini Corporation game, programmed and designed by BJ and Liz O'Connor."

"It wasn't their fault . . ." Harper began, but the look on Lyons's face silenced him.

"It was their fault," Lyons spat. "They made the game— the game that killed her. And I swore then that I would destroy them!" The police officer turned once again to the sleeping bodies and raised the flat, ugly pistol.

25

THE ATTACK CAME SUDDENLY.

BJ and Liz were following Ariel down a long, echoing corridor, their footsteps ringing off the stone flags, when the creature appeared from behind a tapestry.

"It's grown," BJ whispered, pulling out his knife and holding it before him. "I never made it that big."

The creature resembled a rat. When BJ created it, he had made it the size of a large dog. It was now as big as a horse. It was covered in a fine gray metallic fur, and its flat, slablike teeth were also metal. Its red eyes glittered in the gloom.

Liz jerked her sword free, holding it before her in both hands, eyes fixed on the creature. "I hate rats," she muttered. "I told you I didn't want a rat in this game."

"Where's Ariel?" BJ wondered, looking around desperately. "Ariel," he called. "Ariel, where are you?"

"Forget about her," Liz snapped. "Help me with this thing." She was watching the rat advance. "Tell me why you put this disgusting creature in here?" she demanded.

"The rat was designed to drive the player down that side corridor over there." He jerked his thumb over his shoulder. "That's the corridor that leads to the maze, and once you're in the maze it will take forever to get out."

"How do we defeat it?"

BJ grinned. "Simple. All you have to do is wait right there until the rat is in the center of the tiled mosaic pattern on the ground."

The enormous rat inched forward, its metal tail rasping over the stone floor. It opened its long mouth and hissed. Its red eyes were fixed upon Liz, drawn by the reflections in her metal armor.

BJ backed away from his sister, leaving her alone in the center of the corridor, moving slowly so as not to draw the rat's attention. He stopped when his back brushed the cold, damp wall.

The rat walked into the center of the mosaic and stopped.

BJ's knife flashed out, slicing through the thick rope that connected to the heavy circle of metal suspended close to the ceiling. The wheel was designed to hold dozens of candles to light the hall. But the candles hadn't been replaced for a long time, and the metal circle was thickly coated in white and yellow wax. The wheel crashed down onto the creature in a tremendous explosion of sound, pinning it to the ground. Its lashing tail struck sparks off the floor as it attempted to wriggle free, and its squeals sounded like a baby crying.

Liz backed away from the creature. The blow should have killed the rat but it was still alive, its metal-tipped claws scratching deep grooves in the stone floor, its tail thrashing from side to side.

"Let's go," BJ said urgently. "It looks like it's going to

break free! Watch out for the traps."

"I hope I remember them all," Liz muttered.

They raced down the long corridor, Liz's metal heels echoing loudly off the stones. One of the ancient suits of armor that lined the walls suddenly lumbered to life, ponderously lifting an enormous double-handed sword. BJ bent and grabbed the ragged carpet beneath the suit, jerking it up, sending the armor crashing back into the wall. The suit broke up into a dozen pieces, revealing nothing inside.

The corridor narrowed until it was barely wide enough for two people to stand side-by-side. A series of ornate round shields lined the walls, decorated with the faces of men and beasts.

"Ready?" BJ whispered.

"Ready," Liz said.

BJ pointed to the arched doorway at the end of the corridor. "Once we're through the door, the steps will lead into the heart of the dungeons."

BJ went first, counting the shields as he ran down the corridor. As he passed the third shield on the right-hand side, it came alive, an enormous serpent's head rearing out from its center. BJ struck at it with his knife, but the serpent's head turned at the last moment and the boy's knife threw off sparks as it slid off its metal scales. The fanged mouth opened wide as it darted in again—and then Liz's razor-sharp boomerang sliced neatly through the head, severing it completely. The boomerang curled sharply in the air and flew back into her hand.

BJ raised his hand in silent thanks and hurried on. He was ready for the next serpent, striking at it even before it had come out of the shield, and when the enormous bat flapped out of the last shield he cut it neatly in two. Breathing hard, he leaned up against the door at the end of the corridor and rubbed his hands across his smooth head, feeling it slick with sweat. The shields were designed to weaken the players' energy level, but with the virus running through the game, there was no guarantee that the fangs and teeth and claws weren't lethal.

Liz followed her brother down the corridor, moving far more cautiously. The shields on the left side became active only in a two-player game.

A hooded cobra struck out from the center of the first shield. She attacked it with the boomerang in her hand, cutting off the head. It dropped onto the floor, forked tongue flickering. It was still alive. It bit into the girl's boot, its fangs rasping off the metal. Stooping, she caught the head on the end of the boomerang and flipped it into the shadows. If they ever got out of *Night's Castle* in one piece, she swore she would never play this game again.

An enormous scorpion appeared on the surface of the third shield, its tail curled, ready to strike, but Liz kept her distance and swung at it with her sword.

"Snake, scorpion, spider," she muttered as she approached the last shield, with the enormous black spider painted onto its surface. As she approached, the image shimmered and a black hairy spider detached itself from the surface of the shield to leap straight onto her chest! She squealed with fright: she could actually hear the creature's jaws clicking. The metal armor saved her. The spider's legs couldn't find a grip on the smooth surface and it slid to the ground. Liz stamped down so hard that sparks flew from her heels and the spider scuttled into the shadows. The girl's face was chalk-white when she joined her brother at the door. "I want you to make me a promise," she hissed. "No more spiders in Gemini Corporation games."

BJ looked disappointed. "But they're such fun to program and so many people are afraid of them. There's not much point in making a scary game without including a few spiders—and snakes and rats, of course," he added.

But Liz didn't hear him. She was standing at the door that led down to the dungeon, staring into the darkness, her head tilted to one side, listening.

"You won't hear anything," BJ said. "It's as quiet . . ."

". . . as the grave," his sister finished. "Ariel?" she called. "Ariel? Where are you?"

"I saw her go this way," BJ said, crouching down at his sister's feet, looking at the slimy steps that led downward. He could feel a chill, damp wind on his face, carrying with it dozens of unpleasant smells. At least the virus hadn't destroyed that part of the game. Programming a castle was relatively easy; it was the little details like the smells that were extraordinarily difficult. The walls were covered in a glowing green mold that bathed the steps in sickly emerald light. He pointed to the walls. "In our version of the game, the walls were lined with lighted torches," he said, suddenly reluctant to descend into the green-tinged darkness.

"Whatever 'killed' the first players is down there," Liz said, lifting her sword and stepping past her brother. "We have to face it."

"There's probably nothing down there now," BJ said

confidently. He straightened up and dusted off his hands. "Whatever virus lurked in the dungeons has obviously escaped into the rest of the game.

"Or maybe Ariel has managed to defeat it," he added hopefully.

"Game Players."

The voice boomed and echoed off the stones, which distorted the sound and amplified it.

"Game Players. I am waiting for you."

"You're wrong," Liz whispered. "It's waiting for us."

26

"WHAT ARE YOU GOING TO DO?" Harper demanded.

Lyons stretched out his arm, pointing the gun first at Liz, then at BJ. His face was blank and expressionless.

There was the sound of movement in the metal corridors outside, shouts and echoed footfalls, as more police arrived.

"Killing them will serve no purpose. It will not bring your wife back," the Game Maker said desperately.

"I will avenge her death!" Lyons snapped.

"Surely you knew she was a burnout when you married her," Harper said, frantically trying to keep Lyons talking, hoping the other police officers would arrive. He realized that the game had reached a critical stage, could see it flickering out of the corner of his eye, but he couldn't risk turning his head away from Lyons.

"My wife had never played a VR game until she married me."

"Well, then, what made her turn to them?" Harper demanded, his voice rising. "What changed her? How did she get into the games? Maybe you brought them for her to play? You told me yourself you were away when she died. And that she had been dead for a week. Surely you contacted home during that week—you must have phoned home at least once?"

Lyons rounded on Harper, eyes blazing, gun raised threateningly, but the small, stout man pressed on, realizing that he was close to the truth.

"No, you didn't." His voice fell to a whisper. "You didn't check. Maybe if you had, you might have known that something was wrong. Maybe your wife took to playing VR because her husband was never home. Maybe she started playing VR because she was interested in her husband's work. Maybe . . ."

"Stop!" Lyons shouted. "Enough."

In the long silence that followed, a dozen black-clad police officers burst into the room, guns leveled. They halted when they saw Captain Lyons. His back was to them and only Harper could see the tears that sparkled in his eyes. Taking a deep breath, Lyons said: "Everything is under control in here. Secure the area. Let no one in or out."

"Headquarters is demanding a report, sir."

"I'll make my report when I'm good and ready," Lyons snapped. "Now leave us."

The officers saluted and left the room, leaving Harper and Lyons alone.

"I had a wife once too," Harper said very softly, looking past Lyons to where Ariel lay still and unmoving on the metal bed. "Her name was Celeste. She was a great gameplayer. She helped me develop many of the first VR games. And she was one of the first to become trapped in one of them, to fall into a VR coma. That's why the

141

doctors call it Celeste's Syndrome. There was a fault in the game. She died in the VR world—and in this world she fell into a coma from which she never awoke. It was one of my own games," he said bitterly. "Can you imagine what it is like to create a game that kills someone you love?" He stopped, and then nodded. "Yes, I think you can." He took a deep breath and added, "First I lost my wife, and then I was accused of making an illegal game. In a matter of days I had lost everything." He raised his head and looked at his daughter. "Well, almost everything."

"I never knew," Lyons said quietly.

"And I never knew about your wife." Harper turned to point to the screens. "Don't blame the twins. We have no one to blame but ourselves."

Eddie Lyons looked at Harper for a long time. Then he holstered his pistol, and without another word, both men turned to the screens.

27

"THIS HAS TO BE WHERE THE VIRUS STARTED," Liz said as they came down the damp stone steps into the dungeon.

BJ nodded silently. He was appalled by the destruction the virus had caused here, in the heart of the game. In places, whole sections of code had been either destroyed or so altered that the computer no longer recognized them. Parts of the dungeon walls were simply missing, cut away as cleanly as if they had been sliced off with a knife. There was nothing beyond but a gray emptiness that made him feel queasy just to look at it. Much of the code that created the illusion of the ceiling had been so corrupted that bits of it seemed to hang in long jellylike strands to the floor. BJ tapped: it still felt like stone.

They passed an enormous oriental tapestry that should have sprouted a three-headed dragon. The center section, and the wall behind it, was missing and only the dragon's disembodied tail lashed the air as they hurried by.

"Game Makers . . ."

The voice boomed out once again. It was curiously flat and one-dimensional, distorted and muffled.

"Game Makers. I am waiting."

"It sounds as if it's coming from the Treasure Chamber," Liz said, her head tilted to one side, listening.

"That would be right," BJ said. "The Treasure Chamber is one of the most complex parts of the game. Remember, that's where we gave players the opportunity to either carry away treasure, pick a magical weapon, or free the sleeping princess. Their action determined how the game would finish."

Liz nodded. "I remember. If the players chose some treasure, they ended up back in the Twilight Wood. If they chose a weapon, they ended up in the castle. And if they chose the princess, then they had the opportunity to start the game all over again but at a much faster speed."

"If you were going to virus any part of the game, this would be it. If you control this section, you can control access to all parts of the game," BJ added.

"Let's go then." Liz was about to step forward when her twin caught her arm, hauling her back. He pointed to the ground without saying a word.

Directly in front of Liz, the floor simply ceased to exist. Through the hole, they could see shifting gray nothingness.

"I wonder what would have happened if I'd slipped through," Liz reflected. "Where would I have gone?"

"Would you ever have stopped falling?" BJ asked.

Liz shook her head. She didn't want to think about it. Taking a deep breath, she launched herself across the gap, landing securely on the opposite side, her armor clanking. Knowing that if he thought too long about it he wouldn't make the jump, BJ simply ran up to the hole in the floor and threw himself across. He landed right on the edge, his heels dangling over the void. His arms windmilled, trying to keep his balance—and then Liz's arm shot out, catching hold of his jerkin and yanking him forward.

"That might be a nice feature to incorporate into the next version of the game," BJ said with a shaky laugh. Liz's expression wiped the smile off his face. "It was just a joke," he muttered.

A light appeared at the end of the tunnel, flickering yellow torchlight that sent shadows darting up the walls. It had taken Liz a month to program them. She had spent hours watching and photographing the effects of light and shade. At least that hadn't changed; all that work hadn't been wasted.

Something moved across the light, throwing a huge distorted shadow onto the wall.

The girl shuddered. That had no part in the game.

Holding their weapons before them, BJ and Liz moved down the corridor and stepped into the lighted chamber.

The room was cavernous, its roof lost in shadow, its walls buried beyond great piles of treasure. Gold, silver, multicolored jewels sparkled and glittered, throwing back the torchlight, blinding them both.

A shape materialized out of the brilliant light. "I am Night's Master, the Lord of *Night's Castle*. You have successfully negotiated the terrors and dangers of my kingdom." The figure strode forward, the flickering torchlight running off its golden skin, turning its red eyes to spots of fire. The twins saw it was a young man.

"You have come through to my Treasure Chamber," he

said, spreading his arms wide to indicate the piles of gold and jewels scattered around the room. "Now you may claim your reward. You may take whatever you wish as your prize. Choose wisely." The Lord of *Night's Castle* turned and stamped back to an enormous throne of solid yellow-white gold and slumped into it, his elbow on the arm of the chair, his chin resting on his closed fist.

The twins looked at Night's Master. He was modeled on a statue they had seen of a Greek god. He looked about eighteen years old and was six feet tall, with tightly curled golden hair, pale gold skin, and blood red eyes. He was barefoot, wearing a simple white robe tied around the middle with a broad red belt. Night's Master also represented the most complex piece of computer programming the twins had ever attempted; he was capable of making independent decisions based on the information he received.

"Choose," he boomed. "Take your pick of my treasure. Or perhaps you would like a weapon with special powers to help you venture on into my kingdom." When he smiled, Night's Master showed perfect white teeth.

"We are looking for Ariel," Liz said loudly.

Night's Master leaned forward, four frown lines forming on his high forehead. "I know of no Ariel."

"She came down here. Another player," BJ said, "another visitor to your kingdom."

"You are the only intruders into my kingdom." He sat back in the chair, arms draped over the sides. "Choose," he repeated. "Take your pick of my treasure. Or perhaps you would like a weapon with special powers to help you venture on into my kingdom."

"We choose none of your treasures," Liz said.

"We would prefer to travel on," BJ added.

"Choose. Take your pick of my treasure. Or perhaps you would like a weapon with special powers to help you venture on into my kingdom."

BJ nudged his sister. "That's the third time he's said that. He should give us the opportunity of passing into the chamber to the sleeping princess."

"Maybe the virus has damaged his database of phrases."

"Choose. Take your pick of my treasure. Or perhaps you would like a weapon with special powers to help you venture on into my kingdom."

"This room looks fine," BJ whispered. "The virus must be in the room beyond. Pretend to look around, then dart through the door behind the throne into the next chamber." Aloud, he said: "We wish to choose from your treasure chamber."

Night's Master nodded.

BJ moved to the left, Liz to the right, as they circled around behind Night's Master. They picked their way through the treasure, looking at items, lifting them up, putting them down again, moving behind the throne of solid gold. There was a door there, almost completely hidden behind the piled-up treasure. Many of the VR gamers who played *Night's Castle* assumed that the treasure chamber was the end of the game. Few realized that the real purpose of the game was to rescue the princess.

"Look!" Liz hissed.

BJ turned and followed the direction of her pointing

finger. "What?" he asked.

"The ceiling. Look at the ceiling!"

BJ looked up, squinting against the harsh reflected light. His heart lurched when he made sense of what he was seeing.

The room was melting! The golden walls were turning to liquid and flowing into the piled treasure, coating cups and chalices, plates, chests, goblets, swords, shields, spears, rings, and necklaces in thick, dirty yellow sludge. Jewels exploded, bursting like broken glass.

Directly in front of them, the great throne was dissolving, the beautiful carving dribbling away, thick bubbles of metal puddling on the floor, the metal steaming and smoking where it touched the stone.

And then Night's Master rose.

The twins recoiled in horror.

The Lord of *Night's Castle* was melting. His golden flesh was liquifying, his hair was dissolving, running like yellow sweat down his face, his blood-red eyes leaking crimson tears.

His mouth opened, closed, opened again, and when he spoke the words were slow and slurred. "Choose . . . Take your pick of my treasure . . . Or perhaps you would like a weapon with special powers . . . to help you venture on into my kingdom . . . into my kingdom . . . my kingdom . . . king . . . dom." He reached for the twins, spattering yellow droplets across Liz's armor. His hands had now curled into claws; his gums were drawn back from his lips to reveal long, ragged teeth.

"Run!" BJ screamed.

The twins raced through the narrow opening—just as

the entire treasure chamber dissolved into a bubbling yellow mass.

Soft applause greeted them. "I'm surprised you made it this far."

The twins turned and found they were facing Ariel, who was sitting perched atop the glass coffin of the sleeping princess.

The girls' black eyes sparkled. "But I'm afraid you won't make it any farther."

28

"SOMEHOW, WE'RE NOT SURPRISED," Liz said, walking forward, stopping before the girl.

"At first, we thought it was your father," BJ continued, leaning back against the wall and folding his arms. His stone-gray eyes darted around the small circular room. It seemed untouched by the virus. Long, beautifully woven tapestries hung down along the rough stone walls. An incredibly ornate Oriental carpet covered the center of the flagstone floor. In the middle of the room stood a glass coffin containing the sleeping princess. Liz had added that detail, borrowing it from an ancient fairy tale.

"However, once we went into the game this time, your father had no further control over us," Liz went on.

"So it had to be someone inside the game," BJ finished. "And somehow, you never ended up in the same place as us . . ."

"Though you came to our rescue when we were in deadly danger. Obviously you were saving us for something else." Liz walked around behind Ariel, forcing her to turn from side to side every time either of the twins spoke. Liz knew that BJ's relaxed pose against the wall was for show; if she could get Ariel to turn completely around, he could grab her.

And then? She had to confess that she didn't have the answer to that.

"The only question we're left with is, why?" BJ said. "We've never done anything to you, we'd never even met you . . ."

Ariel slid off the coffin. "You destroyed my father," she said hoarsely. Sweat sparkled on her shaven head, trickling down her face. A tiny muscle twitched at the corner of her eye.

"We never knew your father," Liz said in an even voice, forcing the girl to turn around to face her. She ran her fingers down a tapestry, feeling its weave. She wondered how this room had so far escaped the ravages of the virus—and then realized that Ariel alone was keeping it intact by force of will. Glancing sidelong at her, she guessed that the girl was under enormous strain.

Ariel turned her head to look at Liz. "My father has told you he worked with your parents in the early days of VR technology. He was instrumental in developing the organic memory modules. And yet, when he was accused of creating an illegal game, your parents—his friends—didn't even stand by him. They allowed him to be sent to a VR prison, allowed me to be taken away and put into an orphanage, and then they stole his ideas!"

"That's not true!" Liz snapped.

"Oh, yes, it is!" Ariel's voice had risen to a rasping whisper. Large beads of sweat were now gleaming on her forehead and her long tail of hair was matted to her skull. "If your parents had stood by my father, he wouldn't have gone to jail. But they wanted him sent away, they wanted to steal his ideas. And now you're rich, the most famous Game Makers in the whole world, while my father and I live in a sewer pipe on the Quays."

BJ inched closer to the crystal coffin. The only way out of the game was to open the coffin and kiss the princess. If the game was still working properly, then the player would be given the opportunity of restarting the game at a higher speed or finishing it completely and exiting VR.

Ariel rounded on him. "Stay where you are!" she snarled. She turned back to Liz. "So I decided to pay you back, pay you back for all the years of suffering, pay you back for the years that my father spent in a VR prison." She was visibly trembling now.

Behind Liz, the pattern faded from the tapestry.

"So I took your new game, and I introduced an intelligent virus into the organic memory. First, I went into the heart of the game, into its most complex structure, and I took the game code apart. Then I reassembled it with the intelligent virus buried so deeply in the code that it was invisible." Ariel spun around to look at BJ. "But I am part of the machine. I *am* the machine. I discovered that not only could I control the game, I could also control the virus. Once I knew I could do that, I infected a dozen copies of the game and released them onto the market. And then I waited."

"You waited for people to fall into VR comas!" Liz said in horror.

Ariel dismissed that with a shaky wave of her hand. "It was the only way I knew to get you to run. I knew you'd want to go into your game and try to fix it." She started to laugh, but it came out as a hoarse rasp. "The rest was easy." The carpet at her feet faded to a dull gray. "And now you're here. And you will remain here for the rest of your lives, in the living death of a VR coma."

"Ariel," BJ said desperately, "you've got to get out of here . . ."

"Oh, *I'm* going." Ariel smiled, showing her teeth in a savage grin.

"What happened between our parents happened a long time ago. Before we were born. I don't know the truth of what happened. But I do know our parents were killed and your father is still alive. And if he had been working with them in the complex on the moon, then he too would be dead."

"And if our parents destroyed your father, then why did he offer to help us?" Liz demanded. "Why did he say they were his friends?"

"I know what the virus is," BJ said. "I recognize it by the way it operated on the Treasure Chamber, melting it."

"If you leave us here," said Liz, "you're condemning all those people in VR comas to death."

"That makes you a murderer," BJ snapped. "Your father never made an illegal game in his life . . ."

"Do you think he'll be proud of what you've done?" Liz finished.

The tapestries and carpet vanished entirely. The flag-stones lost their distinctive color and turned flat and gray. Then the walls began to melt, the gray stone turning liquid, sliding down the walls, puddling on the floor in sticky globules.

"You've lost control of the virus," BJ shouted. "We've got to get out of here."

"It's destroying you," Liz said. "Look at you! If you don't get out of the game now it will burn you out!"

"I . . . am . . . in control," Ariel said hoarsely. Closing her eyes, she threw back her head . . . and detail flowed back into the room. The melting stone walls were strong again, and the carpet and tapestry reappeared on the floor and on the wall.

BJ launched himself forward, catching Ariel around the waist, wrestling her to the floor.

The room melted.

The ceiling vanished, the walls dissolving like a wax candle, huge gaping holes appearing in the floor.

Liz tried to open the crystal coffin lid before the virus warped and destroyed it, but it was stuck fast. BJ staggered to his feet, holding a limp Ariel in his arms. He thrust her toward Liz, then drove the pommel of his dagger into the coffin lid. The crystal shattered.

"BJ," Liz whispered, "if this doesn't work . . ."

"It'll work," BJ muttered. He leaned over and kissed the princess. If he ever got the chance to rewrite the game, this bit was definitely going!

The white-haired princess opened her eyes . . .

The room vanished.

29

CAPTAIN EDDIE LYONS SIPPED a glass of ice-cold water and gazed down over the city. From this height it looked almost beautiful. Night was rolling in from the east, and the sky was purple and yellow on the horizon, lights blinking and sparkling in the sulphurous fog.

He was in the twins' penthouse apartment, and at this height it was possible to see some of the brighter stars, invisible from the streets below. Looking at them, Lyons wished he knew their names. He turned as a door slid open and Liz and BJ O'Connor strode into the room.

"This is a surprise." BJ grinned.

The captain put his drink down. "I thought I'd come and tell you myself. All the charges against you have been dropped."

"And the coma patients?" Liz asked, perching on the arm of a leather sofa.

"Recovering," Lyons said. "BJ identified the virus correctly. Once we had that, it was relatively easy to bring the victims out of the coma."

"And Ariel?" BJ asked.

"She is still receiving treatment. Her central nervous

system was put under a tremendous strain as she attempted to hold together the VR world against the ravages of the virus. Harper is working with the doctors now, providing computer implants that might replace some of the damaged nerves."

"What will happen to her?" Liz asked.

"I don't know." The police captain shook his head. "That's not my decision. There'll be a trial, of course."

"All those things she said . . ." BJ began.

"Were not true," Lyons said. "I checked the records. Your parents did everything they could to keep Harper out of jail. Ariel was mistaken."

"I'm glad it's over," Liz said softly.

"Is it true you're withdrawing *Night's Castle* from sale?" Lyons asked.

"Absolutely. Neither of us could ever play it again without some frightening memories," Liz said.

"But do you know what was the most terrifying part about *Night's Castle*?" BJ asked.

"What?" Lyons asked with a smile. "The werewolves, the lightning, the giant rat, the melting rooms, the Night's Master . . . ?"

BJ shook his head. "Waking up and finding you looming over us!"